HEALING THE VETERAN

CIARA KNIGHT

If you purchased this book without a cover you should be aware that this book is stolen property. It was reported as "unsold and destroyed" to the publisher, and neither the author nor the publisher has received any payment for this "stripped book."

ISBN-13: 978-1-335-23015-7

Recycling programs for this product may not exist in your area

Healing the Veteran

Copyright © 2025 by Ciara Knight

All rights reserved. No part of this book may be used or reproduced in any manner whatsoever without written permission.

Without limiting the author's and publisher's exclusive rights, any unauthorized use of this publication to train generative artificial intelligence (AI) technologies is expressly prohibited.

This is a work of fiction. Names, characters, places and incidents are either the product of the author's imagination or are used fictitiously. Any resemblance to actual persons, living or dead, businesses, companies, events or locales is entirely coincidental.

For questions and comments about the quality of this book, please contact us at CustomerService@Harlequin.com.

® is a trademark of Harlequin Enterprises ULC.

Love Inspired
22 Adelaide St. West, 41st Floor
Toronto, Ontario M5H 4E3, Canada
www.LoveInspired.com

Printed in U.S.A.

And he said unto me, My grace is sufficient for thee: for my strength is made perfect in weakness. Most gladly therefore will I rather glory in my infirmities, that the power of Christ may rest upon me.
—*2 Corinthians* 12:9

To the wounded heroes—human and canine—
who have given so much of themselves
in the name of service and sacrifice.

Chapter One

Jolene Pearl closed the black leather-bound Bible with gold embossing and set it on the hospital rolling tray. The patient's monitor beeped and bleeped in the evening light that slid through the plastic blinds. A soft snore indicated a painless sleep, so Jolene tucked the covers up a little higher on the woman's frail frame, catching a sweet whiff of lingering perfume that dulled the antiseptic odor of the room.

Hopefully, the woman wouldn't wake and need something. Jolene wouldn't wish the feeling of being unable to move and facing the darkness alone on anyone else. Not after... An injection of ice shot through her veins. No, she wouldn't slide back into a fifteen-year-old trauma. She'd moved past that a long time ago.

Shadows under the door indicated nurses busied for their shift change. It wouldn't be long before they shooed her out with the end of visiting hours, so Jolene accepted she had no choice but to leave; otherwise, if given her preference, she'd remain with the woman until she took her last breath.

With a heavy sigh, she shuffled out into the bright light of the hallway, shielding her eyes for a moment until they adjusted. Familiar faces behind the nurses' station waved, so she offered a friendly smile, then boarded the elevator.

Morning would come early with chores before evaluations and then therapy sessions. Nana's Hippotherapy and Horsepark for children with mental and physical disabilities had boomed—a shock considering it met resistance from Willow Oaks town residents in the beginning, led by Ace Gatlin. A man she couldn't figure out.

"Hold the elevator."

Jolene threw her arm out to keep the door from closing and waited for Sheriff Angelina Monroe to jog down the hall and join her.

The small-framed but strong—and sometimes intimidating—woman adjusted her belt laden with many protective devices slid into pockets and loops. "You reading to the patients again?"

"Yes, and you? Were you here for work?" The elevator lowered, leaving Jolene's stomach a floor up.

"Work, I'm afraid."

They stepped off the elevator and out the sliding doors into the fresh fall evening breeze. Jolene could almost smell the aroma of pumpkins and cinnamon in the air. Probably carried from the new bakery that opened in town. Everything in Willow Oaks, Georgia, embraced autumn with a welcoming hug.

"I hope nothing serious," Jolene said.

With the sun below the horizon, darkness blanketed the parking lot, but a white light shining down from a post like a spotlight on her car led the way. A few of the rays splattered onto an SUV with *Sheriff* written along the side.

"Nothing more than usual." A bark echoed in the parking lot from the sheriff's cruiser. "I had to stop by to get a statement from a suspect who claimed an officer used excessive force." She pointed at her vehicle.

"I guess he won't mess with a K-9 unit again."

Sheriff Monroe shook her head. Her hair didn't move since it was tied back in her military-style bun, but her glossy pink lips spoke of a more feminine side. "Unfortunately, our canine friend here wasn't on duty at the time. Not that the suspect was actually injured beyond slicing his own hand open trying to jimmy the lock of an abandoned building for him and his friends to play with snap bangers."

"Snap bangers?"

"Yeah, the things that you throw on the ground and they make a snapping sound like a pistol." Sheriff Monroe opened the back gate of her SUV and pointed. "I'm afraid Bear here is in some real trouble. It's a shame since he's normally so sweet and gentle."

A tingle of warning slid along Jolene's skin, but curiosity won. Inside the cruiser, she discovered a cage with an ears-down German shepherd. A jagged scar along his front flank where a leg once was tugged at Jolene to move closer.

Her heart double-tapped, then stopped. Wounded? Sad? Alone? "Is there anything I can do to help?"

"If you know anyone who could take him in, that would be amazing. He needs a home. His handler was killed in the line of duty and he struggles with PTSD."

"Dogs get PTSD?" Jolene asked, nudging a little closer.

"Yes, and he has a bad case. The poor guy is calm and sweet unless something upsets him. I tried to take him home, but after this incident I can't have him around my small children."

Warning sirens went off in her head. "I would take him, but I can't since I run the hippotherapy program for Hudson and Juniper, and I live in an apartment over their barn."

Sheriff Monroe held up her hands as if surrendering. "Not asking that at all." She unlocked the crate and snapped her fingers, but the animal didn't move.

"Then what exactly are you asking?" Jolene took a step back, retreating to her car before she did something impulsive like buy a house and quit her job just to help the poor K-9.

"Just let me know if you think of anyone that might take him in that doesn't have children. Preferably someone who doesn't have much company while Bear is in his rehabilitation phase." Sheriff Monroe petted the black-and-tan animal, who opened his runny eyes. And at that moment, Jolene understood the old saying about puppy-dog eyes. Her chest tightened at the sight, and instead of a full retreat, she joined the sheriff in petting the dog.

Jolene chuckled. "Sheriff Monroe, there's only one person that meets that description."

"Call me Angelina, please." She held up the dog's face by his chin and the animal let out a whine. "Who's that?"

Oh dear Lord, help me. I can't walk away from this poor wounded animal.

"Ace Gatlin," Jolene blurted.

"Say what?" Angelina laughed. "He doesn't like anyone, does he?"

"I know, it sounded funny when I said it, but now that I think about it... Mr. Gatlin doesn't want anyone around him. He's a recluse. And isn't that what Bear here needs?"

Angelina tilted her head and eyed Bear. "I've seen Ace only a few times at important town events at which he vocalizes his opinion and then vanishes."

"I know. I've tried to invite him to the farm to work with me on improving his mobility and strength for his prosthetic leg, but the most I've gotten out of him is a grunt or a door shut in my face."

Angelina took a step back and eyed Bear. "Don't take that personally. He's like that with everyone."

Jolene sighed. "Don't take it personally? I'm the one who runs the program he led the charge to stop. I think it is personal."

Angelina offered a tight-lipped smile. "I'll head out there as soon as I'm done here and ask him. It's better than letting the poor animal be put down."

The police radio blared. "Dispatch to Sheriff Monroe."

She held up one finger and went to the driver's seat. "Sheriff Monroe."

Jolene sat on the tailgate at the dog's side petting his soft yet coarse coat and thinking about how his mobility must be a challenge for him as well as the loss of his partner. She also mulled over what Sheriff Monroe said about Ace. She'd already been rejected countless times trying to reach out to him. She'd even tried to get him to volunteer at the Kenmore farm to help children with physical disabilities by demonstrating the benefits of the program. And also to sneak in some much-needed therapy for his leg.

Stroking the animal, she focused on the area with fur growing back around the scar and only registered a few words coming from Angelina's radio, like "Fight in progress" and "10-4."

Angelina appeared once more with hands on hips. "Gotta go."

Jolene rubbed Bear's ears, her insides melting and churning. "What will happen to him if Ace says no?"

Angelina toed the ground, concentrating on a cracked piece of the asphalt. "I can't take him back to my house tonight so I'm out of options. I'm afraid that Bear has one strike for aggressive behavior, and if he gets another one, the state says we put him down. No safe place means he'll be euthanized."

Bear jolted onto three legs, hopped down, stumbled, then settled into a puppy sit next to Jolene's car as if he knew she'd already lost the internal battle on what came next. "Looks like he knows I can't let that happen."

"If you could at least try to speak to Ace, that would be a huge help. I'll take this call and check back in with you later." Angelina handed her a bag of food and an old, smelly bed, then shut the back of her cruiser. "Sorry, he tore into his good bed." Before Jolene could manage a good argument, Angelina took off in her cruiser.

Jolene didn't know what else to do, so she opened the back door of her car, and Bear hopped in, turned once, then collapsed with his chin resting on his one front paw.

With a heavy sigh, Jolene settled into the driver's seat, cranked the engine and drove toward Ace's farm. "Well, maybe he takes to animals more than people?"

Even she didn't believe that, but what choice did she have except to try? So she drove out of town and passed Kenmore farm to the turnoff a few miles later. Her car rumbled and jerked along the gravel road. Bear whined, and she worried that perhaps the jostling hurt his amputation. Certainly Ace couldn't turn away a fellow wounded warrior in need. They both had lost a leg in the line of duty. This had to be a God thing.

She pulled up in front of the house as close as possible so Bear didn't have to walk far, turned off the engine and opened the back door, but he didn't budge. A crinkled brown leaf fluttered onto the back seat, but he didn't even look at it. As if he'd shut down from the world again. Poor thing. "Okay, it's probably better that I explain before you go up there anyway. Ace might just frighten you with his gruffness."

She shut the door and followed the perfect brick path with flowers dotting each side to the large farmhouse with periwinkle shutters. She approached a beautiful white-trimmed front porch complete with a swing on each side. Definitely not the typical image someone would have for the home of an ex-marine hermit.

If a man kept a place this nice, there had to be a heart in there somewhere. With a tight swallow, she knocked on the door and turned away to make sure that Bear was okay.

Not a sound inside the house. Maybe he wasn't home. Though he was always home except for the occasional appearance for local governmental business or checking in on his feed store in town. Never a social call to anyone and barely a grunt or a wave to passersby. She peered through the front window, but not even a shadow moved so she faced her car once again as if to see whether Bear had an idea.

She'd have to spend the night in her car with him somewhere because she wouldn't be able to take him home. At least the weather was pleasant. In the morning, she could come back and try again.

She turned on her heels with her hand raised to knock one last time but found Ace towering over her. The door hadn't squeaked or anything. She sucked in a quick breath and stumbled back.

The man stood well over six feet. Dull light shone through the open door around him, highlighting his farmer muscles and thin waist. A scar slid down from his brow along his temple, but it didn't distract from his handsome face. Dark hair skirted his eyebrows, accentuating the deep lake-blue eyes.

"You knocked," he said, the words falling from his lips with mechanical precision, void of any warmth or curiosity.

She shook off her apprehension, cleared her

throat and regained the one step she'd backed away. "Yes. I apologize for disturbing you, Mr. Gatlin, but I need your help."

His brow rose, causing the scar to thin. "What's wrong?"

"Oh, sorry, it's not for me. It's for someone else who's been wounded. He's having a tough time and—"

"You've got the wrong person. I'm no good to help anyone." He retreated over the threshold.

Was that sadness that caused his lips to droop and his gaze to drop? "No, sorry. I'm not doing this well."

"Doing what well?" He stopped and tilted his head as if to analyze her answer.

She straightened her button-up and lifted her chin. "I'm not here to ask you to help with a person."

"Then what are you here for?"

A bark stole her attention, but she snapped back to catch Ace shutting his door. She shot her foot into the way. "If you'd just listen."

He swung the door wide and crossed his arms over his chest. "I don't need a dog. I've got cattle and horses and goats. I'm not an indoor-pet kind of guy."

"One second, please." She raced down the steps and swung open the car door, certain if

Ace saw the wounded animal he'd welcome him into his home. "Just meet him."

Ace descended the stairs but remained on the brick walkway with a distant glower. Bear plopped down on the seat and dropped his chin to his front paw.

"Looks like we feel the same way about this so point made." Ace nodded toward the drive. "Best get going."

No, she wouldn't give up that easily. "It's here or he'll be put down."

A brush of fur to her leg drew her attention to a black-and-tan blur moving faster than she'd guess Bear could maneuver. He was even too fast for Ace to block his entrance. And she thought the high school star linebacker could block anything.

"Get it out of here," he ordered.

She walked up the front porch steps in time to catch a glimpse of Bear tumbling to a stop and settling in front of a large fireplace in the main room. He put his head down and looked at them with those eyes that could melt any person.

Except Ace.

"Go," he ordered, pointing outside, but Bear only closed his eyes and groaned.

Jolene saw her opening. "Listen. If you don't

take him, he'll be euthanized. I'd keep him, but I can't because he's not safe around children due to PTSD. His handler died. He's served and now they want to put him down because he can't reacclimate to society. Sheriff Angelina Monroe had to take a call so I agreed to bring him here. He's missing a leg and I thought—"

"And you thought because I'm an amputee we'd instantly bond over being less of a man?"

"No. Less of a man? You're not lesser. I think there's plenty of you." She waved her hand at him but heat rose up her neck to her cheeks at her words.

He returned to crossing his arms over his chest with a bicep-flexing move. "Plenty of me?"

"I mean..." She shook her head. "I'm saying that this poor little guy needs help, and you're the only one that can help, so for once maybe you shouldn't be so...so..."

He leaned his shoulder against the doorjamb and crossed a slippered foot over his other. "So what?"

She closed her eyes and pinched the bridge of her nose. *Come on, get it together.*

"I'm not a dog person, and I don't want to rehab some sick animal. I have too much to do on this farm as it is, not to mention running the feed store."

She dropped her hands by her sides, her temper making a rare appearance. "You can't be that selfish." With a spin, she held her arms up at the opulent house he hid inside. "You have all of this and you won't even share it with a dog?" She wanted to also say he was a miser who only cared about himself, because only a man without a heart could try to take the Kenmore farm from an ailing old lady—something Ace had attempted a few years ago. A sore spot with her employers, who were fast becoming her family.

"You can tell Sheriff Monroe that her trick to send the prettiest girl in town to convince me to open my heart didn't work."

Jolene opened her mouth, then shut it. Pretty? He thought she was pretty? "Angelina didn't convince me, I volunteered. And don't try to distract me with empty compliments."

"I don't do empty anything." He stepped aside for her to enter. "So take your dog and go."

She let out a huff and brushed past him into the heart of his home. A place more sterile than the hospital. Sparse furnishings, little to no personal effects and immaculate. She was pretty sure he'd pass the white-glove test. Not what she'd expected, yet he was ex-military so maybe that part of him had been permanently tattooed into his personality. "Come on, Bear."

Nothing. Not even one eye opened. She squatted. "Listen, you can't stay here." She stole a look over her shoulder at the man who stood by watching her like a hawk homing in on prey. "How do you feel about sleeping in a car tonight? Come on, I won't let them put you down, promise."

"Of course you won't," he grumbled.

"What's that supposed to mean?"

"You're a person who spends all her time helping others instead of facing her own issues."

She stood and glared at him. "What's *that* supposed to mean?"

He lumbered to her, abandoning the open door. "Don't know what caused you to be this way, but let me save you some heartache and pain. You may not have figured this out yet, but you can't save everyone so you should stop trying."

"That's cynical."

"That's life." His chest rose and fell, and if she didn't know better, she'd think she saw a flicker of emotion behind his iron wall barricaded with ten feet of proverbial baggage.

"Better than hiding from the world to keep yourself safe from getting hurt." She shouldn't be saying this to a wounded person. He needed her empathy and understanding. All her therapy training screamed at her to be patient and polite and think about what his needs were, but what about the dog's needs?

"There she is." He cracked a half grin.

"There's who?" she asked.

"The woman behind the therapist." He strutted past her, stealing the oxygen from the room, but she managed to remain standing.

"Are you trying to imply that I'm a clinical and cold person?"

Bear let out a groan and stretched his paw a little farther.

"No. I'm saying you don't know how to have a friend, only how to take care of someone. I've seen how you spend every waking moment helping others. What did you do in your past to cause you to have to make up for it?"

She opened her mouth. Nothing. She wasn't trying to make up for some past misdeed.

He didn't allow her a chance to respond before he gave her a dismissive wave. "He can stay the night."

Her pulse calmed and a blast of relief flooded her. "Thank you. Thank you. Thank you."

"I'm not agreeing to anything. It's late, and you need to leave. The dog won't move. Don't see much of a choice. Come back tomorrow after your therapy sessions end to pick him up."

She took a step toward him and he blinked, his gaze soft as it swept over her face, but then his jaw tensed and he pointed to the door. "It's late. Please leave."

"Right." She hurried out before Ace changed his mind, but she couldn't help but think about what he'd said. Not about being pretty—because that didn't matter since Ace Gatlin had the emotional availability of a deer tick and would never be relationship material—but about her being there beyond the therapist. Did she do that? Did she treat him like a client? Maybe that's why he'd never agreed to work with her.

Tomorrow, when she returned, she'd devise a plan to not only convince him to keep Bear because it would be good for them both but also how to get him to open up more. He needed to return to life instead of hiding from it, and she'd figure out a way to knock down that wall even if she had to blast through it.

Why he'd bothered her with his accusations of making up for something in her past was absurd; it was others who'd turned their backs on her. But what he said was telling. It didn't take a trained psychologist to read the pain and regrets in his words. Ace Gatlin suffered from remorse over something in his past. And she'd help him face it—not as his therapist since he'd never agree to that, but as his friend.

Ace jolted awake. Sheets plastered to his sweat-slicked skin.

Breathe. Breathe. Not real.

A deep inhale released the tightness in his chest, and the ache in his leg eased. He ran his fingers over the shrapnel scar above his kneecap and dared to lean far enough to reach the empty space below.

Darkness clawed at him along with something sharp. He wiped the sweat from his hairline and turned on the light, regaining his senses. Every morning, the same thing. 4:22 a.m. would forever haunt him. The time of day he'd failed his men.

A squeal drew his attention to the other side of his king-size bed. Fur rose and fell, then a yelp. He didn't need to be a dog to know the poor mutt's struggle. His thrashing stung Ace's heart because he knew the poor creature fought to save the one he'd let down.

Bear barked and woke. His body tensed and he jumped to attention growling at a shadow in the corner of the room. Jolene was right, this dog didn't belong around children, or anyone, any more than he did. "It's okay, buddy," he said in his softest tone.

Bear growled and snapped. Slobber dripped from between his sharp canines.

"Shh, it's okay. I understand. I, too, have those dreams. The kind where you try so hard to change the outcome but never can."

Bear's lips lowered and he licked his muzzle, then settled down with a whimper. Ace dared to reach for him. Bear army-crawled a paw length closer and leaned into his palm. "You know you shouldn't be in my bed." Ace eyed the smelly bed with holes in it. "Then again, I don't blame you. I think you need an upgrade."

Wind whipped outside, squealing through the screen. Bear angled to face the noise as if ready to attack the threat. "What do you think about eating an early breakfast?" Bear hadn't touched his kibble last night so Ace thought maybe he had more sophisticated tastes. "I have a steak in the fridge."

Bear's ear tweaked back, then forward, and he tilted his head, let out a bark and darted from the bed.

A thud and a yelp drew Ace to throw off his covers, grab his prosthetic leg and hurry to the stairs to discover Bear at the bottom on his side. "You okay, buddy?"

The dog looked up at him with that frustrated expression Ace knew all too well. "I get it's tough, and I have this thing." He knocked on his faux leg. "Maybe they make puppy prosthetics."

Bear got up, leaning on his one front paw.

"Don't be jealous. It doesn't fit well and it hurts. You're better off without it. At least you have three legs to stand on still."

Bear tilted his head to the side as if trying to understand his words. Ace reached the bottom and Bear sniffed his prosthetic, then sat back on his haunches.

"You still want that steak?"

"Woof!" Bear bolted through the main room to the kitchen, skittered sideways, his claws scraping the hardwood, and then he fell on his shoulder, got back up and kept going.

"You need to slow down or you're going to scar my floors. Took two days for me to refinish them." Ace hobbled into the kitchen, throwing his hair back away from his face.

Bear waited in front of the fridge, drooling. "We need to work on that, too. No need to put slobber all over my house either. It's a good thing I have a strange attachment to your savior. She has a way of…softening me."

Ace removed the cooked steak from the fridge and chopped it up. "Not that I'd ever tell her that. Or consider a relationship with someone like her, or anyone for that matter. You see, I don't do relationships. Not even with dogs, so this is temporary."

The wind howled again, warning that a storm would be brewing, so he'd need to get out and tend to his chores earlier than normal. But he wouldn't be going into town to check on the feed store today. Not with a dog here with no crate. His house could very well be torn apart when he returned, and he couldn't take him into town with his unpredictable behavior.

Bear groaned and lowered his head, looking up at Ace with those big, dark eyes.

"Don't look at me that way. Nothing you say or do is going to change my mind. I'm no good for you if you have any hope of healing. I don't fix things, I break them. Especially people and, by extension, animals."

He tossed the rest of the steak onto a plate and put it on the floor, started the coffee and headed for his jacket to tend to chores. Bear devoured the steak, then followed at Ace's heels.

He opened the door and Bear bolted through the opening and slid down the stairs, unable to get his legs to brace him the right way.

"Woof."

"Well, that's one way to do it, but you might want to work on a little more grace."

Thunder rumbled in the distance so he eyed Bear, remembering Jolene mentioning his PTSD, but the dog didn't flinch. "Well, if you're coming, let's go."

Ace went to work. He'd found a long time ago that physical activity helped stifle the anxiety that sizzled under his skin. For over two hours he worked on mucking stalls, fixing tackle, brushing down the two horses that he hadn't sold to Hudson Kenmore after breaking them.

He'd been against the hippotherapy program, worried it would bring in all sorts of strangers to his town and big business would follow. Years ago, he'd tried to buy the farm so he could make sure Mrs. Kenmore could remain. He was worried she'd sell to some corporation that would ruin the land and kick her off it, especially with her real estate tycoon son always lurking around. Turned out his worry had been unjustified for her grandson, though. Apparently, unlike his father, Hudson had a heart.

Bear chased his tail, a blowing leaf and a squirrel until he wore himself out and collapsed with his head resting on his paw, watching Ace.

The sun never made an appearance through the dark clouds, so Ace had no idea how much time went by while Bear lay in the corner watching him. "You know, you have three paws. Why don't you help?"

Bear hopped up and barked at the barn door. "That's not helping."

Tires crunched on gravel, drawing Ace to the door, where he discovered Jolene pulling up. "So you could make a good watchdog. That's something."

He wiped his hands and looked down at his stained work clothes. Why did she have to show up here now? He retreated into a stall and pretended to work so that he could put some distance between them, knowing he stunk like manure. And a girl like Jolene, with her blond hair and big blue eyes, tall, thin and perfect, didn't need to be around him.

"Looks like your ride's here." Part of him wanted to tell the poor dog he could stay. If he was totally honest with himself, he enjoyed the company this morning while the rest of the world slept. But Bear would be better off elsewhere with someone more capable of helping him. "She must've found you a new home."

Bear's head turned to look at him, then to the door, and then he backed into the shadows and hunkered down as if he wanted to hide from his new home.

"Hey, anyone in there?" The soft voice of Jolene beckoned his attention, but he knew better than to allow himself to look too long at her or he'd struggle ever turning away again. He'd never be the man she deserved, so instead of crushing her heart, he denied his.

"Working." He was able to make the one word sound steady, but he wasn't sure he could manage much else. The way her cheeks had pinked when she'd spoken last night had accentuated her soft, flawless skin. It had taken everything he had not to study her like a beautiful sculpture in a museum.

"Right, well. I came to see how last night went before my first client arrives." She sauntered in with blue jeans, button-up shirt and boots. All perfectly fit and distracting, so he stuck the pitchfork into the hay and hit his own foot with a thud. Guess there were benefits to not having a real leg after all.

"In there." He pointed the handle of the pitchfork toward the corner of the barn. "Rough night. Had some bad dreams." That was the grossest understatement ever. The poor thing suffered night terrors so real it seemed he lived his worst memories every night over and over again. Never able to escape the truth of his failures.

"Hi there. How you doing, boy?"

Ace stole a look between the stall slats to watch her squat before Bear, but the dog gave no response.

"Not doing too much better, huh?"

For a second, Ace thought about calling Bear out on his theatrics—he'd been chasing things and playing not too long ago—but no need. He was entitled to his moods. They'd been earned after what he'd been through. "He perked up a little earlier, but then when you drove up, he went into there."

"Well, I'll try not to be offended that no men on this farm want to see me." She looked over her shoulder.

Ace stumbled back into the stall door with a clamber. Busted.

"I have to get to work, but I'll check back this afternoon. Hopefully by then, I'll find someone to take him. If I had a place, I would, but since I live in that apartment above the barn, I can't."

Irritation scratched at his own mood. "You don't stay in the main house? What kind of people are they? That old apartment isn't fit for anyone."

"They renovated it. Even has air-conditioning and running water. All good." She stood and came over to the stall door, propped her arms on it and rested her chin on her hands.

"Why would you care? You don't like me, remember?"

"Never said that. Just don't need anyone bothering me," he shot out before he could confess how much he really did like her. He'd be as clumsy as that beast in a Disney movie he'd watched one night; it tried to win the girl's heart by fumbling around like a fool. But unlike that fictitious character, he was a real beast inside. Too gruff and too full of anger to have a woman around.

"Well, I'll go so I don't bother you anymore." She pushed from the door and wiped her hands on the backside of her jeans.

"It's time for you to face the fact that you can't fix everything," he blurted.

She rounded on him and marched forward, close enough to smell the hard labor on him, so he shuffled away. "Challenge."

"What?" He set the pitchfork aside, straightened and shoved his hair from his eyes.

"I said I challenge you."

He froze, feeling like he'd entered a field of traps. Somehow she was working an angle. Everyone had an angle. "What are you talking about?"

"A friendly challenge between friends. You say I can't find a home for Bear, I say I can."

She smiled, a sweet, I'm-gonna-win-this kind of smile. "If I can find him a home, then you'll agree to letting me help you with your gait."

"Now you want to be my friend?" If the woman wanted to play games, fine, he'd call her on it. What would be the one thing to make a pretty, sweet girl like Jolene leave him alone? "Dinner."

She'd back down. No woman would agree to have dinner with him—his scars, missing leg and winning personality always drove people away.

As he'd suspected, her mouth fell open. "Watch out for the horse flies."

She snapped her mouth closed. "Dinner would be lovely." She took a slow, deliberate step toward him, mouth curved into a grin and eyes full of glowing mischief.

A horse neighed as if warning him to retreat, but he'd stand his ground.

"I'll have dinner with you if I'm unable to find another home for Bear by the end of the day. And if I win, you let me work on improving your gait."

He narrowed his eyes.

"Scared?"

"Never."

She shot her hand through the stall slats so he shook it. "Deal?"

"Deal."

"Should've known you'd pull a stunt like this to get your therapist hooks in me. Just can't help yourself."

"Oh, that was only part one of my challenge. You see, I'm going to be your therapist and your friend."

"You can't be both," he ground out. There were doctors and nurses and then there were friends. He didn't deserve any of them.

"Did I mention I like to take long walks at sunset with my friends?" She sashayed like a dancer on stage out his barn door.

Ace rounded on Bear. "I blame you."

If he didn't know better, he'd think that dog smiled.

Chapter Two

Jolene led the last horse for the day out into the corral. Jimmy Samuel held tight to the reins. The little man had recovered from his physical trauma so quickly, but his fear of life still locked him away from the rest of the world.

"You're doing great. Don't worry, we'll take it slow."

Jimmy kept his eyes straight forward; after spending months in the hospital recovering from multiple injuries from a tractor accident, he'd had difficulty reintegrating into society. Something Jolene could understand. But hopefully, with this program and the new friends he'd make at the farm, he'd be back to running around with a smile soon.

If only she could make Ace smile.

After three laps around the corral, Jimmy loosened his fingers from vise grip to tight hold and he looked to his mother at the fence. He lit up and waved before he realized he'd let go of the horn and grabbed it again, but his smile remained. "Look at me, Mama!"

She waved back. "You're doing great."

Ace could criticize her desire to help people all he wanted, but this was proof that her work mattered. That she could save people from a fate of isolation and despair.

After the fourth lap, Jimmy's core gave out and he began to slouch, so Jolene led the horse back to the stall and helped him dismount down the stairs. He opened his arms, and his mom swept him up in a huge hug. "You were so brave."

"Was I pizza brave?" Jimmy blinked up with hope in his eyes reminiscent of Bear's in the car last night.

Jimmy's mother settled him on her hip despite his being too old to be carried; that was a discussion for another day. Jolene appreciated the mom not wanting to make her son struggle with his leg braces, but the more he moved, the better off he'd be. "I think that could be arranged." She mouthed "thank you" to Jolene and swiped a tear from her eyes.

Jimmy hadn't even made it inside the fence the first day, and now he was on the horse. True progress. Hudson and Juniper's little girl, Gracie, waved from her standard spot at the edge of the front porch where she'd be standing at the beginning and end of each session waiting to see if she'd be next. Her pink galoshes toed the edge of the top step.

Jolene's assistant, Mindi, rushed out. "I've got her. You need to get to Ace's and convince him to keep Bear." Mindi took the horse's reins.

"But don't you have a date with Pastor John tonight?" Jolene asked, eyeing Mindi's new boots.

She shook her head. "No, my youngest sister has a play."

"He could always go with you," Jolene nudged, but she knew Mindi would never cross the friendship line with the town pastor. Although, she'd been walking the edge of friendship for months.

"No, it's a family thing." She rushed off and Jolene guessed it was more to escape any further Pastor questions than to get to a play for her little sister. The woman deserved a gold star for raising all her siblings, working and going back to school. That's probably why Jolene got along with her so well. There's camaraderie among workaholics.

Jolene went to sit on the top step with Gracie. "I'm sorry, hon, but I need to make some calls before I head out. I promise tomorrow morning before school, I'll take you for a few turns around."

"I am big girl. I ride by myself." She stuck her thumb to her chest.

"You are, but you still need a spotter." Jolene held up her hand and stuck her little finger out. "Pinkie promise."

She nodded twice, and with her left hand, she pulled her pinkie from the rest of her fingers, then hooked it around Jolene's. "Pinkie promise."

Gracie had come such a long way with her therapy, and that warmed Jolene's heart. A little girl on the autism spectrum with sensory issues so significant it challenged her daily, who at one point could only speak in clipped two-word sentences, toe walk and bounce all the time, she had started pre-K in an inclusion class.

Of course, that fact had been lost on Ace when she'd tried to convince him to work with her the first time. The man had resisted all attempts to get him to engage with others.

"Good news, though. Mindi is in the barn and would love to have your help," she said with a pat on Gracie's head and a smile. She took that as permission to leave her top step, leaped off and raced to the barn.

Jolene stood and removed her cell to check

her messages. All of them read the same as the ones she'd discovered on her lunch break—no one was open to taking in a problem dog right now. She sighed and headed to her apartment to grab her car key. But once she reached the room at the top of the stairs, she sat on her bed and eyed the phone. Her heart heavy in her chest, she thought she'd tumble over when she walked to the car. "I can't let them put you down."

Her chest tightened. Could Ace have been right and she had to face not being able to help someone? No. There was always a way. That's what therapists did—they accommodated and adapted for their clients.

Maybe she could find a place in town to live that would take dogs. She'd have to be cautious, but it was the only option. She'd have to find day care or someone to check on him while she worked at the ranch. No way would she chance bringing Bear around children with their own issues. If he was to bite one of them, the damage would be both physically and emotionally significant to her clients.

For now, she had to swallow her pride and head to Ace's place to beg him to keep Bear another night because she wouldn't be able to have enough time off from work to search for a place until the weekend.

And the challenge. Dinner. Maybe that was a God thing. She could meet Ace in town and get him to see that he belonged out of his home instead of hiding at his farm. But why did he say dinner anyway? A tickle of worry had her clasping her hands together to pray for guidance.

"Dear Lord, I can see Your work in this—the bond between Ace and Bear. Please give me guidance to help them...and the patience. If only Ace could see that his farm is the ideal location for Bear. I believe through You this will help both of them. In Your name, I pray. Amen."

Feeling a little lighter, she drove the few miles to Ace's farm to find him sitting on the front porch, Bear on the ground by his side. The sun already dipped lower in the sky with the change in season highlighting the entire porch in auburn and golden hues. It looked like a peaceful spot to sip a cup of tea or rock in the swing with a loved one.

He stood and waited at the top step. Would he remain a distance away from her again like he'd done this morning?

But if he disliked her so much, why did he ask for dinner if he won the challenge? Okay, well, he just said dinner; maybe he wanted her to pay for his dinner to be delivered to him or something. She wouldn't put it past him. The man would rather muck stalls than spend time with her.

She swallowed her pride and made her way to the bottom step to look up at the man who towered over her like a piling of a skyscraper, yet he didn't intimidate her. His eyes were soft and a small smile flashed like he had remembered something funny.

He raised a brow at her. "So?"

Did he have to be so smug? "So, I'm not giving up."

He shook his head. "Of course you're not. But I won the challenge. You'll find stuff in the kitchen."

She studied the way the corner of his lip twitched. "What?"

"Dinner. You owe me a home-cooked meal. I'll go show you where everything is so you can get started."

She blinked at him, waiting for the punch line of his joke. "I thought I was supposed to buy you dinner or order you something to be delivered here."

He laughed. "On your salary? No way. Besides, I prefer fresh ingredients and there aren't many restaurant choices in our area that offer that."

She didn't move. Cooking? Her stomach tightened. "The diner serves your fruits and vegetables, you know."

He opened the door and snapped his fingers. Bear trotted inside with what looked like renewed energy, but when they reached the kitchen, he looked at her and then curled up in the corner as if life had been drained out of him instantly.

Ace shook his head, his dark hair falling over his forehead, the tips brushing his brow. "He's playing you."

"What?" She shook her head, realizing she'd looked at his face a second too long.

Ace leaned down, sweeping her hair behind her shoulder, and whispered, "He was just playing in the yard before he heard your car, and this morning he was chasing squirrels before you arrived."

She peered around Ace's shoulder to find Bear still lying like a postsurgical patient with glazed eyes. "Ah, sure."

Ace opened the fridge and pulled out vegetables. "You'll fall for anyone's woe-is-me routine, won't you?"

She studied Bear, and with her years as a

therapist, she could confidently say the dog was suffering. "He's not faking it."

"Really?" He set the food on the kitchen table and said, "Follow my lead." He took her by the hand, warming her palm. "Okay, well, great you came by. I'll let you know how he does tonight."

At the front door, he whispered, "Now sneak back in and watch him." He opened and shut the front door, about-faced and disappeared back into the kitchen.

What was going on? She looked behind her and around the room as if she might find a camera from some television prank show but didn't see anything.

Feeling silly, she did as she was instructed and returned to the kitchen doorway.

Bear chased his tail, then grabbed a ball from the corner and brought it to Ace. He bounced it and then pointed toward Jolene.

Bear's eyes went wide and he slithered into the corner.

"Oh, don't even try it. I saw you having fun." She strutted past Ace and squatted in front of Bear. "Why are you playing games with me?"

He popped up and tilted his head in that sweet-dog way of his. "Okay, I get it. You want to stay here and don't want me to take you away."

"Woof."

She stood and faced Ace. "Well, guess you have a new dog."

"Wait, what?" He set a knife on the table and eyed Bear, then her.

"You made your point."

"Yeah, that you can be played by people who want you to help them."

"No, by proving me wrong, you showed that he feels so at home that he doesn't want to leave. And I've got news for you." She walked up to him and placed her hands on his shoulders. Wow, he was tall, considering she had to stand on her toes despite her five-nine height. "I know it's scary, but I have to tell you that you're a dog person."

"No, anything but that."

Was that a smile on his face?

Bear grabbed the ball and wagged his tail by her side. "I'm afraid so."

"That doesn't mean you get out of making dinner." He pointed to the table.

She lowered to her heels, hands by her sides, and toed the floor. "One problem with that."

He grabbed some meat from the fridge, then two glasses that he filled with iced tea. "What's that?"

"I don't know how to cook." She held her head up high despite his disapproving gaze.

"What do you mean you don't know how to cook?" He narrowed his gaze as if accusing her of trying to worm her way out of her situation.

Nope, wouldn't give him the upper hand. "You mean because I'm a woman?"

"No, because you agreed to cook me dinner if I won. And I am the victor."

"No, I agreed to provide dinner. You decided I'd have to cook it for you." She eyed the food on the table.

"How can you be an adult and not know how to cook?" Two lines between his eyes made an appearance.

She shrugged. "Didn't have time as a teenager to learn, and I left home shortly after high school, so I never had the opportunity."

"Too busy being popular?" he teased, but she didn't think it was funny.

"For your information, I was an athlete. Played softball, was even offered a college scholarship when I was only a junior in high school."

He placed a cutting mat on the table and then handed her a knife. "So you had ball practice. I played football and was still required to do all my chores and had to cook some nights. Pampered much? Well, Princess, time to learn."

"Do you always assume everyone had an easier life than you did?" She never snipped at her clients, but he brought out the worst in her with his judgments. And he wasn't a client. He'd refused her help. Still, apparently, she should pray harder for patience.

"Most have, but no. I don't think that. I just think that some people focus more on helping others because they don't know how to live life themselves."

She set the knife down, no longer feeling the need to coddle him and coax him into working with her to improve his functionality. But she'd never given up on anyone before. "Maybe you're right. Some people just can't be helped."

He blinked down at her. "I hit a nerve. Sorry, but I just tell it how it is. You spend so much energy and time trying to prove to everyone in town that you're there to be perfect by helping everyone. You can't just be beautiful, you have to be sweet and kind and giving. You get attention for taking care of people."

She recognized the compliment wrapped around an insult causing a bubbling of resentment, but she chose to ignore his dig for now. "No." She closed her eyes and inhaled a deep breath. "I spend my time trying to help others because…because…" She bit back the words she hadn't shared with anyone since she was in high school.

"Because what?"

"Because I'm making up for lost time." She grabbed a green pepper and stabbed it, then drove the knife down to cut it in half. "Cooking wasn't a priority in my life not because I was off playing ball, ignoring my chores, but because I was bedridden, unable to move or even breathe on my own, for almost a year. If I didn't have God to talk to, I would've been completely abandoned and alone. So no, I don't try to play personal helper for some sort of attention-seeking reason. I try to make sure no one ever feels like that. No one deserves to feel alone and abandoned."

Ace's gut tightened and twisted. In bed, alone? Unable to move or speak? Now he felt like the monster he knew everyone believed him to be. "Jolene… I didn't know."

"Now you do." She chopped the bell pepper. If she wasn't careful, she'd cut herself the way she was holding the knife, so he covered her hand with his to stall her movements. Maybe his idea to avoid crowds by having her cook here had been a misstep.

"Please accept my apology. I'm afraid I'm

not good with people. Manners are not my strength." He took the knife from her. "I won't hold you to cooking. You can go." He bowed his head, ashamed of his typical behavior that got in his way in life. It hadn't always been that way, but since that early morning that stole his leg and his heart and his friends, he hadn't recovered. He knew that but didn't have a reason to ever try. And even if he did, he didn't deserve to live a happy life. Not when others paid a price for his mistake.

"No way." She took the knife back. "It'll take more than that to scare me off, Mr. Ace Gatlin. I still have some work to do on you. Now, tell me what to do."

He ran a hand through his hair and eyed Bear, who—if he didn't know better—smiled at him before sitting in the corner. "First of all, you don't cut like that. Here." He held the knife and curled his fingers so that they couldn't be sliced, then slid the knife through the pepper. "Hold your fingers like this so the tips don't accidentally get cut."

She took the knife, but her hand didn't press down hard enough to keep the bell pepper from moving so he stood behind her and put his long arms around her to guide her. "Like this."

She stiffened in his arms and he thought to retreat, but then she relaxed.

"Yeah, just angle your hand a little more." He nudged it into place.

The refrigerator hummed, the ice maker dumped some cubes and the ceiling light flickered. Then everything stopped, or he couldn't hear it anymore. All his senses rested on the fresh fall and apple cider scent of her hair.

His breath came short and shallow, and he realized he had a woman in his arms for the first time in years. How many years? Four? Five? His mouth went dry, and all he wanted to do was remain in that spot for the rest of the night, but he knew better, so he slipped away. "I'll, uh, get the meat going in the pot."

They worked in silence except for the clicking of the knife on the mat and Bear's snoring. When the chopping stopped, he faced Jolene to see tears running down her cheeks. This had been a mistake; he should tell her to leave. Why'd he agree to the challenge anyway? The idea had gone out of his mouth before his brain processed it. He still didn't know why he'd said it. "I'm sorry. What did I do or say wrong?" There was nothing more gutting than seeing a woman cry.

"Nothing," she giggled. "Onions."

His pulse slowed. This was too much. What had he been thinking inviting her into his home to cook with him in his kitchen? It was too...intimate...vulnerable. The last time he'd gone on a date with a woman, not that this was a date, she went to the bathroom and never returned. A setup gone horribly wrong. Despite his friend who had set him up warning her about his scar, apparently it was too much for her to deal with when she'd seen him.

"What?" she asked.

"What?"

"You're staring at me." She scooped the onions together and sniffled, then wiped her eye with the back of her hand. He picked up a napkin from the center of the table and turned her to face him, dabbing at the tears rolling down her cheeks. His thumb grazed her cheek and he found it softer than the petal of a flower in spring. "Don't touch your face. It'll burn your eyes."

"These things will burn me?"

He laughed. "No, your eyes will sting if you get onion juice in them." He took the mat of onions and dumped them into the pot. "Wash your hands."

The water cut on behind him, but he kept his attention on the spaghetti sauce, smushing his fresh tomatoes down until they were crushed.

The aroma of peppery tomato goodness filled the air.

Hopefully, she liked spaghetti; he should've asked. He eyed Bear in the corner. The dog opened one eye as if to tell him he was on his own and then shut it again. Great, some help he was.

"So, seriously? Are you going to keep Bear? Look at him, he's so happy here."

He stirred the sauce a little faster. "Trial. That's all I can promise. I don't know how to care for a dog with his condition. I mean, I fed him steak this morning because he didn't eat that kibble last night. Don't even know if that's okay. Not to mention I'm not the best company."

"I don't know. I think you're pretty good company."

He added some garlic and stirred some more, forcing his goofy grin into submission. Why'd one little remark from her cause so much stirring inside him? "Please, I almost let you cut off your fingers and then made you cry. Not that I haven't had worse first dates." Steam rose from the pot and heated his face.

"Date?"

Sweat dripped down from his hairline and he fought to find the right words not to offend her yet not scare her away. "I—I didn't…"

"Didn't what?"

He turned to find her sitting back in the chair with a huge smile as if she were watching a live show. "You're enjoying this, aren't you?"

"Considering you kicked me out of your house last night... Yeah, a little bit."

"I didn't—"

She sat forward, resting her elbows on her knees. "Quote. 'It's late and you need to leave.' End quote."

"I remember saying the word *please*." He grabbed the spaghetti and dumped it into boiling water, added a pinch of salt and concentrated on stirring and not falling over. By the end of the day, the muscles in his upper thigh cramped.

"That was after you barked and then gave me those same puppy-dog eyes that Bear gives when he wants something."

"I don't give puppy-dog eyes," he huffed.

She stood and walked over next to him, causing the kitchen to heat up a few more degrees. *Get a hold of yourself, man.*

"Whatever you say." She sniffed the pot and looked at him.

"What are you doing?"

"Just seeing if I want to stick around."

He fought the urge to retreat with her so close. "Since I'm your friend, I think I'll stick around to give you cooking tips." She flipped her hair back, drawing his attention to a small scar in the center of her neck.

"You don't even know how to cook."

"Maybe I was just testing you." She winked.

He couldn't read her; every word was a mystery that he wanted to solve. He cleared his throat so he wouldn't sound like a teenage boy when he spoke again. "I saw the way you chop vegetables. If you tried to cook, you'd be down a few digits."

She shrugged. "I'll have you know, I cut my peanut butter and jelly sandwich with exact precision."

He liked this. Standing in his kitchen talking to Jolene. Maybe he could have a friend. Not that he deserved one, but she was here and there was no reason to be rude. Not to mention she'd have to teach him how to work with Bear. "Here, taste this and see if you still want to criticize my cooking skills."

He lifted the wooden spoon and blew the sauce to cool it down, then held it out to her with his other hand under to catch any drips. She opened her mouth and then closed her eyes. "Mmm, okay. I think I'll give you a B on my report."

"B? Why not an A?" He plopped the spoon in

the sink and splashed cold water on his arms to soothe his skin from hot to simmering. Every time Jolene neared him, a weird heat flooded his skin.

"Because of the service."

He grabbed another spoon from the drawer and returned to the stove. "Service? Hon, this is a self-serve kind of kitchen so get the plates out of that cabinet and the forks are in that drawer."

Bear raced over and put his paws on the table.

"Down, boy. Table's for humans. Paws not allowed," Ace scolded.

"Pups gotta eat, too." Jolene handed him the plates and set the forks on the table. "Where's the bread? Can't have spaghetti without bread."

Cabinets squealed open and snapped shut. He'd fix the hinges in the morning. He plated the food, and when the room went silent behind him, he looked over his shoulder to see Jolene standing at the far cabinet near the grand room. *The* cabinet. The one with his greatest regrets.

The plate of spaghetti slipped from his grasp and clattered onto the floor.

He couldn't breathe, but he managed to close the space between them and slam the cabinet door shut. The door to the artifacts of his fallen friends and his buddy who was now in a wheelchair.

His heart hammered and the room spun. Ace leaned against the counter and opened his mouth to bark at Jolene to leave. She didn't belong here. He didn't deserve for her to be in the room with him. Not when he'd caused his friends to die. Why hadn't he died with them?

"Hey, it's okay." Her hand slid to the middle of his back, but he didn't want her comfort. Didn't deserve it.

"Leave," he managed to bark out in between pants.

But she didn't leave. She invaded his space, catching his gaze and taking a deep breath and placing her palm to his heart. A heart that sped faster than Bear chased his tail or a squirrel. But in two breaths, her touch calmed the beat enough for him to find her beyond the blur. Instead of running, she'd remained by his side, without flinching.

Training. Therapist. Patient. That's all he was to her. Another person to fix, to save from loneliness. Only he didn't deserve to be healed. "Leave. Please."

Chapter Three

Ace's gaze went from wide to narrow to lost. Jolene held her hand to his broad, hard chest and breathed slow and steady until his breaths went from ragged to deep.

She ignored his words; she'd dealt with difficult clients before, so she told herself this was nothing new. She recognized that he shoved her away like he did everyone else in his life, but she saw through his iron frame and words to the lost soul buried deep inside. And he needed someone. "It's okay. You're here with me."

He straightened and moved her hand from his chest. "I said leave. Please."

"No." She needed to allow him space to collect himself and take a few breaths on his own, so she turned her focus to Bear, who slurped up noodles and meat. "Well, guess you had a yummy dinner tonight, huh?"

She grabbed some paper towels and cleaned up the rest of the sauce and veggies, scooping them back onto the plate. "Thanks for the help with cleanup on aisle five."

The sauce bubbled in the pot, so she stirred that and then turned it off, not sure if it would burn while Ace continued to grip the counter like he'd break the granite. He was a proud man, so watching him struggle would only make him lash out more. "So what do you think? Two paws up?"

"Woof."

"Great. Guess I'll have to raise my rating to an A, huh?" She set the slobbered, dirty plate into the sink and grabbed a clean one. She plopped spaghetti on two plates and topped them with sauce, then set them on the table.

She dared a quick glance out of the corner of her eye. He'd let go of the counter and now stood with his palm pressed to the door as if apologizing for something. A shrine of pictures and medals and letters housed inside told a story but she didn't get to read it. Her guess was that something that happened in the military took not just his leg but his sense of worthiness. He didn't believe he deserved friends, so he pushed them all away. Good thing she wasn't easy to push around.

"It's getting cold, so I'm digging in." With a twirl of her fork, she took a bite of oregano and basil and tomato goodness. "Wow, I think I just traveled to Italy with one bite. This is really delicious."

"It'd be better if it simmered all day, but I improvised," he said, his voice hollow.

She kept eating, trying not to give him her attention, but Bear licked Ace's free hand dangling at his side. Like a scared animal being coaxed out of the corner, Ace shuffled to the table at sloth speed and settled in by her side.

Bear took his place on the floor by Ace with a gentle grunt. "Glad you like it," he said, a little life returning to his tone.

After he picked up his fork and took a bite, she nudged the conversation in the right direction. "Are you alright? I'm here if you'd like to talk."

"I wouldn't." He took a gulp of his iced tea as if to swallow down the memories. "No therapy. Not tonight. For once, I just want to have a normal meal with someone. Can we just sit and eat together?"

The way he sat, slumped and distant, made her want to pull him into a hug, but she guessed it would be like trying to put her arms around a bucking bronco. "Sure. I'm game." She ate until she scooped up the last noodle.

He set his fork down and side-eyed her.

"Where do you fit it all? You're like the size of a doll."

"You're the size of a mountain, so maybe you don't know what normal is." She sat taller in her chair. "I'm average size, actually a little tall for a girl."

He chuckled. "It wasn't an insult. You know, my favorite gifts at Christmas growing up were the small packages. I think they always have the best surprises."

"Sorry, I'm just me. No surprises." She dabbed her mouth free of any sauce and set her napkin on her empty plate.

"Something tells me you're anything but ordinary."

His words took her thoughts down a dangerous road, so she hung a sharp right. "Maybe you'd find out if you stopped telling me to leave." She turned in her chair to face him dead-on. "You might as well give up because I'm not going anywhere."

He ran a hand through his thick, dark hair and let out a sigh. "Because you're my friend."

She grabbed her plate and went to the sink. "No, I'm only friends with people who want me to stick around. I'll be here every afternoon to see my friend Bear. You might not want help, but he does. I'll be by tomorrow with a plan to work with him on his PTSD. If you don't want him permanently, then we need to get to work so we can rehab him to be rehomed."

Ace looked down at Bear at his feet. "See, we're another client for her to fix."

Frustration bubbled over into a huff. "Stop. Just stop. If I'm here, it's because I choose to be. If I come around because I care, what is the harm in that?"

"What is the harm in that?" He leaned forward and ran a finger down the front of her neck where the vent had been protruding from her skin for months, causing her to shiver under his touch. "Everything. Because some scars run too deep to be seen or healed." He stood and cleaned the dishes, but she wouldn't let him escape that easily.

"You said you didn't want to talk tonight. That's fine, but tomorrow when I come to help Bear, no promises." She took her iced tea and went to the front porch to sit and watch the stars now twinkling in the sky. Bear followed her and lounged at the top of the steps.

A coyote howled in the distance, causing her to lift her head, but he didn't bark, as if the creature wasn't worth his effort.

"Thought you left." Ace joined her, sitting by her side, causing the swing to rock.

"I wouldn't leave before I said goodbye. I just wanted some fresh air. This is my favorite time of year."

"What do you like about it?" he asked with a more genuine tone than she'd heard before.

She shrugged. "The brisk air, the crunching of leaves underfoot, big orange pumpkins and hay rides."

"I have a pumpkin patch on the east side of my property. I can show them to you tomorrow if you'd like. I mean, when we take that friendly walk with Bear at sunset." The way his voice dipped along with his chin made him look vulnerable but struggling to remain open.

"I'd love that, thanks." She stood up and went to the railing to get a better look at the stars. "What's your favorite time of year?"

The coyote howled once more and a chipmunk skittered across the bottom step.

"Used to love winter."

"Why that season?"

He joined her and rested his arms on the banister; bent in half, he met her eye to eye. "Warm drinks by the fire, the crunch of ice underfoot the two weeks a year it's cold enough to freeze, and when we actually get a dusting of snow, it's like waking on Christmas morning."

"Do you love Christmas?"

"Used to. Not so much anymore."

"Why not?"

"It's all commercial and there's no real meaning to it," he grumbled.

"No meaning? It's Christ's birthday."

He shoved away from the banister. "If He's in your heart, I guess you have something to celebrate, but I left God back in the Middle East years ago. Don't see the point in faith anymore."

"How can you deny God?" She wanted to cry at the thought of losing her faith, the only thing that got her through the darkest time of her life.

"Where God came to you in your hour of need, He abandoned me," he said in a hoarse tone.

"How can you say that? Yes, you have a prosthetic leg. And by the way you walk, I'm guessing it doesn't fit well. Why you haven't been refitted is a question for another day, but you're here tomorrow for me to ask you. God brought you home. Doesn't that prove He's with you?"

"No, it proves the opposite because if God was here, He would've let me die and brought the men I commanded home."

The day crawled by. Not even taking a trip into town to check on the feed store helped speed up the day, or when Bear cornered poor

Dave in the back room. Ace worried the man would quit on the spot, forcing Ace to be in town every day to run the store himself, but instead, Dave ended up on the floor rubbing Bear's belly in the end.

When the sun finally dipped lower into the sky, Ace dared to look at his watch for the thousandth time to discover 4:22 in the afternoon. That time haunted him day or night. He froze, staring at his watch until it changed to 4:23 p.m., then he darted inside to shower before Jolene arrived. He didn't want her thinking he never cleaned up.

Not that Jolene had left his thoughts since he'd walked her to the car last night. The woman was a formidable force that didn't give up. But even after showering and putting on his going-out jeans, he had to remind himself she only returned this evening to help with Bear.

By the time he reached the bottom step, Bear waited at the front door, and the sound of Jolene's car and the crunch of gravel sent his pulse into a double tap. He took in a deep breath and promised to keep his cool this evening. They would work with Bear, go see the pumpkins and make a plan for what came next.

Jolene approached with a wide smile and took the steps two at a time holding a large bag. Maybe if he worked hard enough, he'd be able to hop up the stairs like that again. Right now, he doubted he'd even keep up with her on the walk.

He took the bag from her and she squatted in front of Bear. "Hey you, ready to do some work?"

Jealousy nibbled at Ace with the full attention she gave the dog at his side.

"And you?" She stood. "I kept my bargain last night, but today is therapy day for you both." She rummaged in the bag he was holding and pulled out some papers. "Here."

"What's this?"

"Exercises. You expect Bear to do his work, you need to show him you'll do yours. Not to mention, you'll need to keep up with him when he's running around."

"I'm not able to run," he quipped.

"Not with that leg or with the lack of rehab you've done."

"How do you know I skipped out on the rest of my therapy?"

"Because no physical therapist I know would let you leave with a leg fit like that and your gait all wonky."

He opened the door. "Wonky? Is that a professional term?"

"Of course."

"Come on in. You can work with Bear while I take care of some chores."

"Not so fast. Need your help." She snapped her fingers at Ace as if he'd obey her command. He raised a brow at her.

She shrugged and looked up at him with a playful grin. "It worked. You stopped walking away."

He chuckled. "Fine. Tell me what to do."

"I want to check to see if he's hurting anywhere. The vet gave him the all clear to start working, according to the assistant I spoke to today."

He figured she'd be up before dawn working on something. "You found time to call the vet?"

"No, I went by on my way here after I finished at the hospital. I had a patient cancel this afternoon, so I had some extra time."

He shook his head. "And when do you find time to rest?"

"I had all the rest I needed years ago. Now, help me get him to settle on the floor."

Ace eyed the ground and then knocked on his leg. "It's challenging to get up and down low places."

"I can help you with that."

"Never mind, I'll manage." He grabbed the

edge of the sofa, stuck his prosthetic leg out and did a one-leg squat until he plopped down like a toddler.

"Stubborn much?" She patted the floor but Bear remained two feet out of reach. "It's okay, boy, I'm not going to hurt you."

Bear looked to Ace.

"Come on, boy. Mean old therapist won't hurt you."

"Gee, thanks." She sighed and pointed at his leg. "Show me your prosthetic."

"What?" He grabbed the sofa at his side and thought about running, but by the time he managed to get off the floor, she'd be halfway done pulling up his pant leg.

"Come on, you have to show him that I can be trusted."

"What if I don't trust you?"

"Please, I'm a professional."

"That's what I'm scared of. I don't have the best track record with doctors and therapists."

She grabbed his pant leg and dragged his leg toward her. "Not taking no for an answer, so stop being a baby."

He slid the pant leg up a few inches, but she cocked her head to the side and waggled her finger up as if to operate his pants like a puppeteer.

At the edge of where his prosthetic attached

to his leg, he stopped. This time, she scooted in and put his leg on her lap, causing him to fall back against the couch. "What are you doing?"

"Just relax." She pulled the pant leg up, exposing his leg above his knee. "You are one determined man. Nothing will stop you, will it?"

"Not much, no."

"But why do you have to suffer while doing it? You know this doesn't fit right. The swelling in your leg probably went down since you had this temporarily fitted to you. Why didn't you go back for a permanent fitting?"

"No need. This one works just fine." She shook her head, but he tugged his leg away and patted the floor. "See, all good. Come on, Bear."

He army-crawled with a hop each time he had to drag his body forward on his one front paw and his head hung low. "It's okay, boy. I won't hurt you."

He rolled over, exposing his belly to them, so Ace rubbed it while Jolene felt around the joint where his front leg once attached. Then she joined him in the belly rub. "Good boy. All looks good. Now, I'm going to help you with balance while working on desensitizing you to the environment."

"How are we going to do that?" he asked.

"By taking him to different places and introducing him to different situations. First, we're going to test to see what he reacts to and what he can handle. My fear is that a car backfiring could send him into a fit and hurt someone. According to what Angelina told me, loud noises can set him off, and he already has one strike. If he's aggressive toward someone again, he'll be euthanized."

Bear whined.

"Don't worry, boy. I'm here to help, and we won't let that happen." She rubbed his head, then looked to Ace. "Have you dropped anything that startled him?"

"Only the plate of spaghetti."

"What about clapping?"

He shook his head and then grabbed onto the corner of the couch and pulled himself up to sit, then stood with a slight wobble before he found his own balance. To his relief, she didn't baby him by running over and demanding to help him.

"Okay, let's start there." She popped up off the floor, retrieved a leash from her bag, put it on Bear and then passed Ace the handle. "Your job is to take control if Bear freaks out on us. I want to help him, but I don't want to be mauled either. It wouldn't be his fault, but I don't want to take the risk. It's my job to make sure he doesn't hurt anyone."

"Okay." He grabbed hold of the leash tighter and angled his feet so his good foot was forward.

"Ready?"

He nodded. She opened her hands and clapped lightly, then harder and harder and harder until it was loud.

Bear wasn't impressed and put his head down on his paw with a whine.

"Okay, good." She walked behind him and did the same thing again.

Ace remained with a tight grip on the leash, ready to intervene if the dog erupted on her.

They spent the rest of the evening clapping and banging and rewarding Bear for his good behavior but giving him space when he growled. To Ace's surprise, the only thing that really drew his anger was stomping. Especially when Ace stomped at him.

"Okay, so we need to work to make sure if someone runs at him, he doesn't attack, but that's level two. I think we've done enough for today. It's getting late, and Bear looks tired. Tomorrow, we'll take him into town on the leash so he can be exposed to another location. It could agitate him, so we should plan a short trip the first time."

"Town? Do we have to? Tomorrow's Saturday. There'll be a lot of people."

"That's my day off, so it has to be tomorrow. I'm too busy next week with work and reading at the hospital, not to mention working on the grant proposal we need to turn in next month. Oh, and Wednesday, I volunteer to deliver meals to people who are home-bound."

"And on Thursday, you're going to need meals delivered to you because you'll be too exhausted to move."

She waved him off. "Don't be silly. It'll take more than that to take me down."

"No doubt." He unhooked the leash, and Bear raced to the corner and plopped down on the blanket Ace had set out as a bed. "Fine, but we need to go to the pet store, too. He needs a nicer bed and toys. I'm surprised Sheriff Monroe didn't send all Bear's stuff with you."

"She told me that Bear chewed through all the toys she had for him and when he had night terrors he tore his good bed apart."

"Understood, but I don't want that smelly, gross bed in my house any longer."

"He seems happy."

"Not happy enough. He keeps sneaking into bed with me."

She laughed.

"What's so funny?"

"Nothing, just picturing him sprawled out across your bed with you left on the edge with a dog paw in your face."

"You're not far off." He set the leash on the table and went to the door. "Come on."

"Where are we going?"

"Pumpkin patch. Told you I had one on my property. I thought you could pick a pumpkin and take it to Gracie."

"You big old softy. I can't believe people think you're scary."

"I am. You're just too focused on doing good to see it."

He eyed Bear. "You stay here, boy, and get some rest. We won't be gone long."

"I don't think he's going to argue. Looks like we wore him out." Jolene grabbed her jacket and slipped it on. Outside, the sun had disappeared, leaving a moonlit night.

"I didn't realize it was so late already. I haven't even started dinner, but we can heat up some leftovers." He figured he could feed her since she probably didn't have time to eat otherwise.

"Can't stay that long. I have somewhere I need to be tonight."

He opened the truck door and waited for her to climb in, feeling the sting of rejection. "Of course you do. What is it tonight, helping clean out closets at the food pantry, reading to the sick at the hospital?"

"No. I have a Zoom call set up to speak to a veterinarian that specializes in PTSD."

He shut the door and crawled into the driver's side. "What do you ever do for fun when you're not working?"

She looked out the front windshield as if to search for an answer to his difficult question. "I read."

"What do you like to read?"

She looked over at him, her hair falling over her cheek. "Therapy journals and articles mostly."

"That's work." He cranked the engine and drove to the east field. "You're young and beautiful. Shouldn't you be out dating and enjoying life?"

"I could ask you the same question."

"Please, I'm older than you and much uglier."

"Only five years older and more handsome than any of those magazine-proclaimed most handsome men of the world."

He couldn't help but smile. Maybe once he'd been good-looking. Okay, better than good-looking; there wasn't a girl who didn't throw herself at him before he'd been blown apart and wore his brand of loss and destruction for all to see. Loss of his men by his inept leadership. "This mug'll never be on the cover of anything. Now, come on. I have a pumpkin to show you."

He rounded the truck and opened her door for her to hop out and walk by his side. The front lights of the truck shone over the patch, highlighting her long blond hair and silky white skin. Flawless. Both in appearance and heart.

"Wow, look at these." She squatted next to the largest and patted it on top.

"That one'll win the prize for largest pumpkin. I've won three years in a row."

She looked up, batting her long lashes at him, then shielding her eyes from the truck's headlights. "I thought you didn't like to be out with people."

"I don't attend. I send the pumpkin with a friend and we split the prize money. It's not about winning, it's about showing them."

"Well, maybe this year you'll be at the festival with Bear. We could use that as his final therapy challenge. A big crowd like that."

"No, not my scene."

Her lips pressed together and then parted slightly as if tasting the words before she spoke them. "I don't get you."

"I'm not a complicated person. What you see is pretty much it."

"Then why did a man who hated the idea of the hippotherapy program defend me at the town council meeting?"

He thought back to the day when Juniper stood up in front of the town to fight for the Kenmore farm to be turned into a horse therapy program, all so little Gracie would have a safe place to grow up. He'd been shocked to see Hudson at Juniper's side, holding Gracie. It was the first sign the man had traded in his tarnished corporate soul for a real heart.

"I wasn't against the hippotherapy program."

She put her hands on her hips. "Seriously? You had people dressed in anti-hippotherapy shirts."

"It wasn't the therapy, it was the big business. This town doesn't need to be turned into some commercial city. Go to Atlanta if you want that. And you weren't the only one there. Hudson Kenmore was fighting to gain control of his grandmother's land. Didn't want that boy to turn it into some resort, or sell it to his father."

"Hmm…okay. More evidence you need to go out and be around people more, because if you got to know Hudson, you'd discover that the last thing he'd do is turn the Kenmore Ranch into some resort. Besides, you wanted that land long before Hudson and Juniper inherited it. You tried to buy out Mrs. Kenmore when she was too sick to run it."

He eyed the pumpkins. So that's what she thought of him. "I worried the woman might choose to turn it over to her son, the world-conquering Kenmore Global Enterprises founder, and would've been evicted five minutes later. So, I'll stick to my house and send the pumpkins to the fair like I'd planned. Thank you anyway."

"What if I told you I volunteered to help run the fair this year?"

"I'd say I'm not surprised." He shook his head. Why did this woman give so much of herself to so many? She worked a job she barely made any money at when she could be working in a city hospital for much more. She intrigued him.

"Then it also shouldn't surprise you that I get to help with the rules for said contest. I'm thinking it's going to be mandatory for the farmer to be present to win. You know, to share his knowledge and prove he grew the pumpkin."

"You're a sneaky one, aren't you?"

She shrugged and stood in his space. Too close, but this time he didn't turn away. "I'll considerate it."

And he did. As night deepened around him and the house quieted, he found himself replaying their conversations, her words weaving through his thoughts. Despite himself, her proximity earlier had ignited something within him, a flicker of possibilities that he hadn't allowed himself to contemplate in years.

Lying in bed, the moonlight casting shadows across the ceiling, he felt a rare sense of peace settle over him. It was enough to coax his restless mind into sleep, and for the first time in a long while, his dreams were not chased by shadows but filled with light.

He escaped to the town fair, the air thick with the scent of fresh hay and popcorn. He stood proudly beside a giant pumpkin, its orange surface gleaming under the afternoon sun. Beside him was a pretty blonde woman—her smile bright and encouraging as she congratulated him on his win. The applause from the crowd warmed the usual coldness he carried in his chest.

But as dreams often do, the scene shifted, the cheers fading into a silence that felt heavy and foreboding. The sky darkened, and a chill swept through the fairground. He turned to speak to the woman, but she was gone, replaced by an empty space beside him that echoed with a sense of loss.

At 4:22 in the morning, he jolted awake, his heart pounding, a cold sweat clinging to his skin. He found himself on the floor, having rolled off the bed in his turmoil. Bear licked his hand and settled by his side as if telling Ace he understood.

The remnants of the dream clung to him, the fleeting joy and the subsequent emptiness. He lay there for a moment, his breath ragged, trying to shake the eerie feeling that the dream had stirred within him.

Pushing himself up, he sat against the bed, the darkness of the room pressing in. The clock's relentless ticking mocked his discomfort, a stark reminder of the night's passage. With a weary sigh, he realized that sleep would not come again easily so he stood and made his way to the kitchen, his thoughts wandering back to the woman's words. "I'll consider it." Maybe there was more to consider than just the content of their conversation. Maybe it was time to consider new possibilities for his life, to allow more than just pumpkins to win at fairs.

Chapter Four

Jolene's nerves fluttered and flipped her stomach. She told herself that it was all about Bear when she'd put her best jeans on this morning, or when she'd taken time to add some shine to her hair, but if she was totally honest with herself, riding in the truck with Ace by her side headed into town had a strange excitement to it. The last time she'd felt this was in high school when the star baseball player asked her on a date. A date that never happened.

"What are you so deep in thought about over there?" Ace asked.

She jolted out of her fog. "Thinking through possible scenarios to avoid any issues with Bear. I want to make sure this is a positive experience for all of us."

"What else is there to think about? We're going early to avoid big crowds, walking him up and down the sidewalk a few times, then heading back. Simple enough." He turned into a parking space in the heart of town.

Mindi Peterson sat on a bench outside her shop with Pastor John. She couldn't understand why Mindi was so resistant to opening her heart to the man, but she never asked since it wasn't her business.

Maybe Ace was right and Jolene should consider life beyond work and service, but she could never ignore someone in need. God had brought her through so she could serve others. And that's what she'd do, but maybe there was room for both in her life.

"You ready?" Ace asked, slipping the leash around Bear's neck.

"I am. How about you, Bear?" She rubbed under his chin.

His response was a pant and jig in the seat between them.

They exited the truck and met at the tailgate. She scanned the area and pulled a treat bag from her pocket. "The vet told me on the call last night to try to keep him focused on our walk, to train him to respond to me, but I think it's more important he responds to you since he's in your house."

"Okay, just tell me what to do. Never had a dog before." He held out his hand, so she placed the treat bag in it. Her fingers grazed his calloused palm, and she lingered at the feeling of the promise of protection.

His gaze caught hers, so she snatched her hand away. The thought of relying on anyone was too foreign and dangerous to consider. She took care of herself and didn't need any help. A fact she'd learned long ago.

"Tell him to sit, and once he does, praise him and give him a treat to establish the routine and rules."

He eyed Bear and said, "Sit."

Bear obeyed. Obviously, the dog had already been trained well since he was ex-police K-9, but she wanted to follow the specialist's advice. "Okay, now we walk a few feet and have him sit again and offer him another treat."

Ace did as she instructed, and Bear followed with his tail high, eyes trained on Ace. "Now?"

Jolene eyed the street and worried; she preferred her treatment room or the stable or corral. This was out of her element.

"Hey, I've got his leash. He won't get away," Ace said in a reassuring tone.

"I know. It's just if he does have an episode, it could be the end for him."

"That's a lot of pressure to put on yourself." Ace turned Bear around, had him stop in front of her, then crooked his finger under her chin and nudged her to look at him. "For once, share the burden with me."

Her insides warmed at his words and she felt touched. She needed to keep things friendly but professional, and the way her pulse pattered against her neck crossed that line, so she pulled away to give herself some space to think. "Okay, let's cross the street when we reach the other side and repeat the treat routine."

"Got it." Like an expert dog trainer, he kept Bear at his side and then stopped outside the hardware store and had him sit. At the pet store, Jolene waited outside with Bear while Ace went inside then took his purchase to the truck.

They resumed their training by repeating the walk up and down Main Street several times until her nerves settled. "You're both doing great."

He nodded but sweat dripped from his hairline despite the cool temperature outside. His clean-shaven face blotched red and his jaw twitched, warning her he was grinding his teeth. She'd been trained to recognize the signs of someone in pain. "You okay?"

"Yeah, um, what if we stop for a coffee and sit for a bit." He pointed to the diner.

She eyed the people inside and shook her head. "Too many variables. Not a good idea."

He took in a deep breath and eyed the truck in the distance. His hand rubbed his affected leg above where his prosthetic attached and the truth was obvious—he was the one struggling, not Bear.

"Why don't we head back? No sense in pushing things today. Bear did so well." She petted the top of his head but he remained sitting. "Good boy."

"What about me?"

She stood on her toes and mussed his hair. "You're a good boy, too."

"Gee, thanks." He laughed but led Bear by a few people. Jolene made sure to be a barrier between them and the strangers in case anyone jolted or reached out.

One lady—if she remembered correctly her name was Mrs. Chester, the town conspiracy theorist—looked down at Bear as they approached. The last thing they needed was for her to have something to criticize about him, so Jolene quickly said, "Dog in training, please don't touch."

"But he looks so sweet." She leaned over and reached out despite the request.

"Sweet but deadly," Ace ground out, sending Mrs. Chester skittering away with her purse to her chest and a wild look in her eyes.

Jolene scowled up at him. "We're trying to reintegrate him into society. It won't help to make people scared of him."

"I didn't. It's me they're scared of."

She harrumphed. "Right, because you're so scary."

"Smart people are scared of me."

"Are you saying I'm not smart?"

He didn't answer, so she smacked him playfully in the arm, then sucked in a quick breath and waited. She knew better than to make any sudden moves, but to her relief, Bear kept prancing forward, looking straight ahead with the occasional glance at Ace.

At the end of the street, they waited for the crosswalk sign to change. When the light turned to green, they stepped off the curb, but Ace stumbled, his leg buckled and he slammed to the ground. Bear barked and licked at his face.

Jolene grabbed Bear's leash before he could run and glanced down at a red-faced Ace holding his leg, struggling to get off the ground. "Stop for a second."

He didn't stop, so she put a hand on his shoulder. "Relax or the muscles will keep spasming."

"Cars are waiting," he said in a low, angry tone.

"Let them pass." She waved them by, then

squatted next to Ace with a tight grip still on the leash. "Sit."

Bear obeyed and she reached down to massage the spasm from Ace's leg. "If you'd stop being so stubborn and get a better-fitting prosthetic…"

His eyes narrowed, and she realized now wasn't the time to call him out for his poor choices. Humiliation didn't begin to describe the downcast gaze and the tight expression on Ace's face. "Just get me off this ground, fast."

She rubbed the knot just above the connection until it let go and then offered him her hand. "Come on, let's try to get you to the truck."

He gave a short nod and managed to get up on his knee and sweep his prosthetic leg around. With part of his weight on her, he was able to stand, and he hobbled to the truck faster than his leg should've moved.

"Let me drive."

"No, I've got it."

She cut him off and stood in his way. "Stop, tough guy. Ever think of the fact that Bear and I are in the car too, so your stubbornness isn't just affecting you? That leg spasms while you're driving and we could have an accident. Now hand over the keys." She held out her hand and stared him down. An eye-to-eye battle ensued, but in the end, she won and he dropped his keys in her hand, then took Bear to his side of the truck.

Once they were halfway down the road, he slammed his fist against the door, causing Bear to bark. "Hey, both of you, too loud."

"That was humiliating," he ground out.

"Why? Because you fell? Did you never fall in your life?"

"It's not the same thing and you know it." His fists were tight in his lap and his gaze fixed out the window. He wouldn't look at her.

They didn't say another word until they reached his farm. Anger simmered from him to the point it nearly heated the truck. She cut the engine but Bear didn't hop up, so she took advantage of the chance to speak with Ace. "Listen, you won't go back for a leg, but you won't leave the house in fear you'll fall. It's obvious you're stuck, and as your friend, I want to know why."

"If you're really my friend, you won't ask." He shoved the door open and Bear followed him to the house. She went inside to find them on the couch staring at a television that wasn't even on.

She sat by Bear and petted him. "You did

so good. I think we can move on to stage two next weekend."

Ace didn't say anything. He still struggled with falling in public. "You know, you're the only one that can improve your circumstances. No one else can do the work for you. Bear needs you to do better. So do better." She walked out the door but remained for a moment outside to pray when she overheard him say, "Not when pain is your penance."

Bear groaned, plopped down on his bed in the corner of the living room and stared at Ace. "Don't look at me that way." He removed his leg and the cloth to find a spot that had rubbed raw from him overcompensating for the pain. The pages Jolene had left sat on the coffee table in front of him, but what was the point?

"Woof."

"No one asked you. I get it, you rocked your outing and I failed." Embarrassment still crawled around and burrowed deep inside him. But he got what he deserved. No, he deserved far worse. "I know I could've been less grumpy, but you don't get it. You're a dog."

Bear nudged closer and whined.

"Sorry, I know I chased her away and you wish she was still here." He sighed and looked around the room. "Guess I do, too. Just don't tell her that."

Bear shot up and panted, nudging his nose to the papers.

"Fine, I guess I could try. For your sake, so I can take you on walks and stuff." Maybe for them both he could try.

He picked up the pages and eyed the drawn figures and directions. Static gluteal contractions, hip flexor stretch, hip hitch, bridging and pages of others.

Bear trotted over, bouncing with each step, demonstrating he already had better balance, and settled in front of Ace as if cheering him on. "Fine, I'll try, but no promises."

He left the prosthetic on the couch and lowered to the floor. After reading the directions, he determined they all were kid's play. No problem. But by the time he finished all eight of them, he couldn't do a second round. Exhausted, he stayed on the floor for twenty minutes and dozed twice, only to wake up from Bear licking him. "Dinnertime already?"

"Woof."

"Okay, okay." After feeding Bear, Ace checked on all the chores to make sure the farmhands had completed them, left checks in the box in the barn, called Dave to see if he needed anything at the feed store, then returned and did a second set of the exercises. That night, he slept all the way until his typical wake-up jolt.

The next morning, he checked his phone but no messages from Jolene. He told himself that was good; maybe she'd given up on him. She'd be better off without him.

Later that night, Bear whined at the door. Ace let him out to do his business but he only sat at the top step watching the driveway. Day and night two went the same. No calls, no visits, and he told himself it was for the best. He didn't like it. Maybe he'd been too rude.

For three days, he worked hard on the farm and did his exercises four times a day. On the fourth day, he managed a second round twice. On Thursday, after he finished his final round, he hopped into the kitchen to grab a drink but fatigue won and he fell against the cabinet.

When he righted himself, he realized it wasn't just any cabinet he'd fallen into. It was *the* cabinet.

His breath caught between opening the door and running from his past again. He'd put everything in there. The unopened letters from his buddy who also lived but at the price of both his legs. And the pictures of the lost and fallen. The men he'd sent to their deaths.

With shaking hands, he grabbed the knob and opened the door for the first time in a year, excluding when Jolene had opened it.

His heart thrashed against his ribs so hard he thought they'd bruise.

Logan's letters sat in a neat pile, but he couldn't bring himself to pore through them. To read his rants about how Ace had ruined his life and murdered their friends. He was a coward for not facing it, and he would…someday. But not today. Today, he eyed the photo of his men's faces staring back at him in judgment. He took out the picture of all seven of them and crumbled into the kitchen chair before he landed on the floor once more.

Broad smiles greeted him, and for a second, he found himself connected to them like they were still here with him. His men, his friends, his brothers. He scanned the expectant faces from their first day of their first tour together. They'd all thought they were going to help change the world, and they'd counted on Ace to keep them safe, but he'd failed them. He sucked in a gulp of air and couldn't let it out.

He dropped the photo and bent over, his head between his legs. Nausea rolled up inside and he heaved in fiery air. Bear whined and placed his chin on Ace's leg, rubbing against him as if to provide him comfort. "It's my fault, buddy. It was all my fault.

"If there is a God up there, take this pain, please. It's too much." Tears rolled down his cheeks so he swiped them away; he didn't deserve to grieve. But maybe he could do more than hide away on the farm. Yes, he didn't deserve to have a life, but maybe he should take a page from Jolene's book of good deeds and dedicate his life to others. Help those who needed things. What he could do, he wasn't sure, but he knew who could guide him. Only she hadn't spoken to him, and he wasn't entirely sure she'd return on Saturday. No, he was, because of the person she was. No matter how many times he'd been rude to her, she'd come back to help.

A do-gooder. She didn't like the term, but he had no other words to describe her. A woman pure of heart came into his life. A beautiful woman who shone so brightly a hint of her light seeped into his charred heart.

An idea formed in his head to smooth the waters between them. To show her that he wasn't always a brute and could learn to help others with her guidance. "What do you think about going into town to run one errand?"

"Woof." Bear grabbed the leash from the table in his mouth and waited at the door.

That was one smart dog, and he had no signs of aggression. Maybe this had all been a ploy to get Ace to agree to therapy. No, Sheriff Monroe wouldn't go along with something that manipulative, and he didn't think Jolene could either. He drove them to town and parked outside the florist with Bear's leash firmly in his control; he found himself walking better over the curb already. He'd never really done his physical therapy; he wasn't interested when he'd returned home. Now, though. There was purpose behind his efforts. He couldn't save the ones left behind, but he could help those that were here now. And maybe in the process, he could give Jolene a break to live her life.

Mindi stood behind the counter arranging a pot of flowers. "Well, hello there." Her usually blue hair had been muted to a duller brown, probably something to do with the fact that it was obvious she liked the pastor in town. Not that she should have to change herself to be worthy of him.

"Hey, um, good afternoon," Ace stammered. "I thought you were working at the Kenmore ranch with Jolene."

"I am part-time, and I work here part-time

until they secure the next grant for the hippotherapy and physical therapy programs. I'm working toward becoming an assistant someday, though."

Bear pranced over and leaned against her until she petted him. Flirt.

"What can I do for you both?" she asked.

"Come." Bear raced over and sat down, so Ace gave him a small treat the way Jolene had shown him. "Stay." Ace eyed the area full of so many different flowers he wouldn't know where to start. "I'm not sure."

"No worries, I can help you." She wiped her hands on her apron and came around the counter. "Is it for a friend or a love in your life?"

"Friend," he said a little too fast and too hard.

"Right." A knowing grin curved her lips. "So what does your friend like?"

He thought about it but had no clue what flowers she liked. But women liked this kind of thing, right? "Fall." It was all he could come up with.

She lit up. "I have the perfect thing for you." She went over to a round of buckets and lifted a bouquet of rust, orange and bright yellow. "What do you think?"

"Perfect."

Bear lifted his head as if to confirm Ace's assessment.

Mindi picked up a glass vase. "I can put these in here and tie a bow around it."

"No thank you. I'm going to use one of my pumpkins as a vase."

Mindi put the vase down. "That sounds amazing. Would you mind selling me some pumpkins and letting me steal that idea?"

"For what?" he asked.

"A wedding. Since Mrs. Harrison is semi-retired and I can't afford to buy her shop, we have an agreement. I started my own floral business venture where I buy the flowers from her at a discount, arrange them and deliver them for events."

He shrugged. "Two part-time jobs aren't enough? I can see why you and Jolene get along."

She rang up the flowers and he paid, then took Bear's leash in hand.

"Thanks so much."

"Thank you for the idea. Hey, do you have thirty pumpkins about this size?" She cupped her hands in front of her.

"I think so. Won't all be the same, though."

"Even better. It'll make it more natural since it's an outdoor wedding. How much?"

"Call it a gift. I have more than I need or could ever sell. I'll bring them by tomorrow when I come back into town with Jolene to work with Bear. Don't know what time, exactly, though."

Mindi pointed out the window. "If you need to confirm with Jolene, she's over at the ice cream shop with Gracie and Juniper. I think they came into town to order some specialty items through the hardware store."

He ducked behind a display. "No, um, it's all good." His pulse revved. Now wasn't the time. If he was going to grovel and apologize for his behavior, he didn't need an audience.

"If those are a surprise, you can go out that door."

Right. The flowers. He didn't want to explain that it wasn't—or say anything at all—so he slipped out the back without another word, Bear at his side. But when they rounded the building and Bear spotted Jolene, he barked and barked. Ace had to drag Bear to the truck while trying to stay out of sight. Ace managed to get Bear into the truck, crank the engine and speed out of town like a coward.

His phone dinged but he didn't look at it until he reached his home again.

Avoiding me?

Great. He'd tried to make things better and only mucked things up worse. "What do I text back?"

Bear shook his head.

After a deep breath, he typed, No. Bear was agitated so thought it best to get him back to the truck and head home.

It wasn't technically a lie. Bear did get agitated...to see her. He could understand that. His blood pressure had risen at the sight of her, too.

Then you won't tell me to leave if I show up tomorrow before lunch?

I'll have something ready to eat. There, that would work. He could have a nice meal and tell her that he'd like to help and that he'd been rude and apologize in the privacy of his home.

No. Taking Bear out to lunch for step two.

He tossed the phone to the side. "Great. Now I get to humiliate myself in public. No. Not happening." With nerves kicking up, he took Bear inside and went to retrieve thirty-one pumpkins. He cleaned them up and scooped out the insides of the one perfect one. It took all evening, but by the time he fell into bed, he had the arrangement done with a few wildflowers added from the backyard to make it more natural looking.

And in the morning, when he woke up at 4:22 without screaming or clawing his way out of the dream, he rose and made coffee. He worked all morning feeding and grooming animals, checked on his farmhands, harvested some vegetables and cleaned the house free of dog fur. No matter how much he worked, he couldn't calm himself, though. His nervous energy kept him moving, but it wasn't like his typical anxiety; it felt more energetic than terrifying. A strange fluttering like bat wings took up residence in his stomach, making it hard to eat anything all day.

When Jolene's car finally appeared in the driveway, he took two deep breaths and went out to meet her. Ready to be a put-together, calm and focused gentleman. But when she stepped out in a dress and boots, her hair pulled up and makeup highlighting her eyes, all thoughts fell from his head.

Chapter Five

Bear stumbled down the front steps but didn't fall this time. Progress. "Hey there. How's it going?"

Jolene looked up to find Ace standing, mouth open, but not moving. "You okay up there? Catching those horse flies?"

"Yeah, um… Didn't know we were dressing up." He stood back and held his hands out, looking down at his long-sleeve button-up that accentuated his strong arms and his normal, non-ripped or -stained jeans.

He looked good. Too good. She brushed her hands over the soft skirt, realizing what he meant. "Right. I had an event this morning and never found the time to change."

"I could go put on better clothes."

"Why? You look nice, too." She joined him on the top step and straightened his shirt. The royal blue was reflected in his eyes, capturing her attention. "This looks good on you."

"Uh, thanks. You, uh, look pretty."

"Thanks." Awkward silence fell between them. He fidgeted and pulled a piece of tiny lint from his pants.

"Ready?" Jolene eyed Bear, who tilted his head in that sweet way of his that made her want to hug him.

"No," Ace blurted but then cleared his throat. "I mean, can you come inside for a moment?"

Why was he acting strange, like he was nervous or something? The normally grumbly man with short words and even shorter tolerance for people welcomed her into his home like a gentleman.

Bear ran in as if to coax her to say yes, so she did. "Okay. But I can't run too late. I have to be at the hospital at four for my shift."

"Right, I'll make it quick so I don't keep you from anything important."

His words shot true and straight and honest. The man thought he didn't deserve anyone's time or attention. She snagged his hand just inside the door and looked up at him with the most serious face she could. "You're important."

His mouth opened but then shut. He stepped aside, but to her relief, he didn't grunt or pull away; instead, he laced his fingers between hers and moved a step closer. "I hope this shows how important you are and shows you I'm grateful for your help with Bear. And that I'm sorry for my rudeness last Saturday."

Bear sat next to the table as if presenting her with the most beautiful bouquet of flowers in fall colors displayed with a pumpkin vase. "Wow, that's beautiful. Did you make that?"

"Woof."

"Not you, silly." She dragged Ace closer and, despite wanting to keep hold of his hand, she released him to pick up the pumpkin.

"Yeah, well, Bear helped pick the best pumpkin out of the bunch. It's my way of apologizing for being so gruff the other night. Honestly, I'm surprised you returned. I mean, I know you had to for Bear."

Her chest tightened. Did she share why she'd really returned? Sure, partly for Bear, but also for Ace, and not just because she wanted to help him. "Friends don't abandon friends."

He flinched but recovered. "Well, I hope you accept my apology."

"As long as I get to take these flowers with me, I'll accept anything you say." She set them back down on the table. "Can I leave them here until after lunch so that I don't mess them up?"

"Sure." He shoved his hands in his pockets

and toed the floor without losing his balance. "Actually, if it's okay with you, I need to drop some pumpkins off to Mindi."

"Really?"

"Yeah, she said she thought my idea was perfect and wanted to use them for some wedding. Did you know she has her own business making floral arrangements and delivering them to events on top of her two part-time jobs?"

"Not surprised. She's a hard worker and has a family to take care of." Jolene glanced down at the flowers. "No one's ever given me flowers before. I mean, not unless it was for being sick." Her parents had sent them instead of visiting the hospital. A store-bought, didn't-even-pick-them-out kind of gift.

His brow tightened and he shook his head. "That can't be true."

She chuckled. "Well, from what I understand, I did get some flowers when I first ended up in the hospital." No, she wouldn't dampen the mood with that story. Not when she was enjoying Ace's company so much. She liked this side of Ace Gatlin. Tall and proud with a hint of humility and softness. Not that he'd want anyone to think that about him. "Let's go."

Bear hopped up to race down the stairs and was waiting next to the truck by the time they reached it. "So what happened yesterday to set Bear off?" she asked.

He opened the passenger-side door to the truck, but she waited for him to answer. "I may have exaggerated slightly. When I saw you there I was at the florist, and I panicked."

"Why?" She stepped back to allow Bear to hop into the truck.

"Because I didn't want you to see the flowers before I put them together. And I wasn't sure if you would even speak to me after last Saturday." He studied the button on her jean jacket for a moment too long.

She blinked at him, reading his pressed lips and soft face as embarrassment or regret. Therapy reading of patients wasn't an exact science. And if she was honest with herself, the vision was clouded by their friendship. "Why would you think that? You struggled, but that's part of healing."

"But you didn't text or call all week."

"I was giving you space because I'm your friend, not your therapist." She climbed into the truck while he went around to his side and got in.

"Friends can call friends whenever they want. They don't need a reason." He cranked the engine and the truck rumbled to life. "I mean, Bear was upset he didn't get to see you all week."

She cupped Bear's face and said, "I'm so sorry if I didn't come visit. I had to finish that grant proposal, remember?" Did Ace really care that she hadn't spoken to him? Had she misread his needs? How many times had she picked up the phone to call him or driven over for a visit only to decide he needed room to figure things out without her pushing him?

"Right. Of course." Ace drove them past Kenmore Ranch. "I know I asked this before, but what do you like to do as a hobby? Besides read."

She patted Bear on the neck, buying some time to think about his question. "Hobby? Hmm...not sure I've ever had one of those. Well, besides walking with my friends."

He nodded and rotated his hands around the steering wheel. "What about when you were a kid?"

She pressed her lips together and eyed the world outside. "No, hobbies weren't encouraged when I was a kid. I had a strict schedule my nanny kept—exercise, school, homework, softball practice and music lessons."

"Sounds busy. No wonder you're always working. Music can be a hobby, though. You play an instrument? Enjoy listening to music?"

"No, and only the kind on the radio. I know I should gush over Bach and Beethoven but after being forced to study them ad nauseam, I'm more of a radio kind of gal."

He drove into town and stopped at the other end to park near the diner. "We'll have to figure out what you like to do for fun."

She shrugged but didn't have any desire to really figure out what she liked to do for fun on her own. She didn't even like being alone much. The quiet always got to her. "I like doing this for fun." She pointed at the diner up the street.

"Thought we couldn't take him into the diner."

"We can't. We're picking up a picnic lunch and going to the park. There'll be other dogs there, and people as well."

He opened his door, grabbed binoculars from behind the seat and hung them around his neck.

"What are those for?"

"No time like the present to try a new hobby." He lifted the binoculars. "Bird-watching."

She laughed and walked to the diner. "Wait here, you two. I'll be right back."

She raced inside and picked up her to-go order. Mrs. Chester sat on a nearby stool next to her husband. "Still got that mutt, I see."

"He's actually a hero. A wounded hero."

Jolene's hackles rose but she softened her tone. "We're working on retraining him. He's the sweetest thing. I'm so sorry if I offended you the other day." She'd always found kindness worked the best when dealing with injured egos.

"I wasn't offended. Concerned." She nodded to Mr. Chester. "We want to keep our residents safe, and Ace said the dog is dangerous."

Jolene rolled her eyes. "Please, you know how Ace is. All bark and growling."

They both nodded. She didn't like putting Ace down and thought to correct her words, but the lunch order plopped down on the counter in front of her.

"You know, town says you're spending a lot of time with that man. Something going on there?"

Jolene stiffened. She couldn't deny there was something going on there, but what, she couldn't define. "We're working together to rehab Bear since he dedicated his life and his leg to protecting all of us. He was wounded in the line of duty, so I think Ace has a vested interest in helping a fellow hero."

Ace would never call himself a hero, but if Jolene's suspicions were correct, the man tortured himself because of losing someone, and he probably risked his own life to save them.

"Right, well, just be careful." Mrs. Chester turned back to her husband as if to get his opinion on the subject, and Jolene took her opportunity to exit fast. She joined Bear and Ace and ushered them away from the café and far from the Chesters. No need to stir up trouble. "Let's go."

"You didn't have to buy lunch. I would've made it for us," he offered, but she waved him off.

"Thought you'd be busy with harvest season and all that."

"Plenty of ranch hands to do the labor. And even with my long days, I probably still get more rest than you."

She sighed. "Not that again. Let it go. I'm taking time off now to hang out with a friend."

"As his therapist."

"Can't I be both? Your friend and his therapist?" She guided them around the diner to the park at the center of town where a blanket and drinks in a cooler waited under a beautiful oak tree filled with golden and auburn leaves.

"Who did this?" he asked.

"I dropped it off after my meeting, before heading to your place."

"Of course you did." He shook his head and eyed the flannel checkered blanket.

She put the basket down and held her breath, but she needed to nudge him past his will to not try because he thought he deserved to suffer. A topic she'd address at a later time. "I can help you lower."

"Nope. I've got it."

To her shock, he did manage to get to the ground with less effort and didn't even fall.

Pride fluttered in her chest. "Look at you. Someone's been doing his exercises."

"Maybe. Someone had to if they were going to help a certain someone with all her good deeds before she lands herself in bed from exhaustion."

"I'm fine. Stop worrying about me." She yawned, only proving his point.

"I thought if I helped and did my part with the exercises, maybe you'd try to rest a little. Maybe spend some more time with your friends."

She handed him a bottle of water and poured some into a dish for Bear. "Got any specific friends in mind?"

"Well, you have the three-legged kind." He pointed to Bear, who slurped up water.

"I'm his therapist, and you said I can't be both, so who's the friend you're thinking about?" She wouldn't let him out of saying it.

If he wanted to spend time with her, he'd have to admit it to himself and her. She'd had enough emotionally unavailable and long-distance people in her life.

He leaned back against a tree, took a swig from his bottle, then sat forward again and took her hand in his. "I'm not going to keep you from the life you deserve, so I won't pretend that we have any sort of future together, but I wouldn't mind spending some time with you, my friend, when you're not otherwise occupied. That means if I help free up your schedule a little, you'll have time to hang out."

"Hang out?" She slipped her hand free, crossed her arms and eyed the picnic lunch she'd hoped would show him he was worthy of friends and possibly more. But maybe he didn't think of her in that way.

"I didn't mean it like that."

"No, it's fine. I get it." She set out the sandwiches and the chips and the fruit, busying herself so that she didn't have to face him, but he crooked his finger under her chin to make her look at him.

"You deserve so much better than me. It's selfish of me to even ask you to be in my life as a friend."

She swallowed the rising lump and closed her

eyes, relishing his touch. His palm slid to cradle her cheek so she leaned into his hand. "What if I might want more than friendship someday?"

She opened her eyes. "When you're ready."

He retreated back to his side of the blanket. "I couldn't ask that of you because I don't know when or if I'd ever open my heart to more than friendship."

"Why?" she asked, longing to draw that passionate, giving person she saw inside him out into the world.

He picked up his sandwich and studied the lettuce hanging over the side of the bread. "Because I can't. That's all."

"Because you won't let go of guilt for something I'm guessing wasn't your fault."

His face turned red and he shot up straight. "Don't."

She wanted to push, to make him open up to her, but the way his nails dug into his sandwich, causing holes through the bread, meat, cheese and lettuce, she knew he'd only run if she nudged him any further. "Okay. I won't. Let's eat."

"Thank you." After a couple of breaths, he took a bite. "Mmm, this is good."

Bear whined.

"Don't worry. I've got something for you."

He sat up and panted with excitement.

She removed the cling wrap and set the plastic plate of hamburger on the ground for Bear to dig in.

"Well, he's happy," Ace chuckled. "Thanks for this. But seriously, you don't have to pay. You've done so much already. Look at him, I can't believe that they wanted to put him down for aggression. Besides his bad dreams, he's the most tame and obedient animal I've ever encountered. A big teddy bear."

"Maybe so, but I spoke to Sheriff Monroe, and we still need to file a report within sixty days. I told her my idea about the festival and she agrees that could help with the notion that he's been rehabilitated and cancel their plans to euthanize him. She's handling the red tape with the state. That festival will be our last obstacle. An event full of people. If all goes well between now and then, Bear should be out of danger."

"Then we'll do that. The two of us."

"Woof."

"Sorry, the three of us," Ace said.

They spent the next couple of hours throwing a ball for Bear and sitting on the blanket looking at birds through the binoculars. He pointed at a bird that looked pretty. "There's one."

She looked through the lenses, then to him. "What kind of bird is it?"

He chuckled. "No idea. Bird-watching isn't my hobby."

"No offense, but I don't think it's mine either."

They both laughed and decided to watch Bear instead of birds. On occasion, one of them would lean into the other as if on a date, but that was as close to *beyond friendship* as they managed. Finally, Jolene eyed her watch and packed up the wrappers and empty bottles. "Sorry, I have to be at the hospital at four so I need to head back to your place to get my car and flowers, then home to change."

"You could skip volunteering for one night and have another cooking lesson instead." He and Bear both gave her puppy eyes.

For a second, she thought about neglecting her duties to have some more fun, but she couldn't. Not when anyone could be alone and needing a friend. "Not fair if you both gang up."

Ace sighed and picked up the cooler and bag of stuff, while she carried the blanket. At the truck, Hudson waved from across the street, then jogged over. "Hey, glad I ran into you. One of the farmhands that works both our lands wanted me to tell you that it appears that someone cut your fence wire on your west side."

Ace huffed. "Really? Great, I hope Benjamin Snyder isn't still hunting on my land."

Hudson shrugged but looked to Jolene. "You headed to the hospital?"

"Yeah after I pick up my car from Ace's place, I'll run by the ranch to change and finish up paperwork and then head to the hospital."

"I can take you. I'm meeting Juniper and Gracie there. She's seeing an audiologist. I took a walk because Juniper said I was in the way. I didn't like that Gracie was upset. I'm headed back to pick them up."

"That's kind of you, Hudson, but as Jolene mentioned, her car's at my place. I'll make sure she's at the ranch to finish her work for you." Ace's tone sounded curt and challenging.

Jolene cleared her throat and nudged her elbow into his ribs but the man stood tall with his chest out as if having a manly showdown with Hudson.

The two men did this silent conversation thing with eyes and jaw twitches until Hudson offered a nod and stepped away. "If that works best. I'll see you at the ranch for dinner." He walked away and Ace grunted under his breath.

"You still don't trust him, do you?" Jolene asked.

Ace opened up the door to his truck for

Jolene to climb in. "Man has to earn my trust. And I don't like how you're overworked. They take advantage of your dedication."

He joined her in the cab with Bear between them and started the engine.

"They don't take advantage of me at all. Actually, Juniper and Hudson are always urging me to take time off."

"Then you should. A little time off would be good for you. Maybe give you more time to discover a hobby you like or to spend time with friends."

"There is a lot to do to get the program to where it is in the black, but I'll think about it if you think about being more open to trusting Hudson and Juniper."

"Fine." He drove them down Main Street toward his ranch but Jolene couldn't help but wish she did have more time to spend with him and Bear. "I'll admit, though, I hear he's good with Gracie."

"He's the best with her. And like I told you, he's done nothing but support Juniper's ideas for the ranch. I don't see him ever building a resort on the property now."

Ace only nodded, and for once in her life, she didn't want to go help someone. Her selfish heart wanted to stay with Ace and Bear, but to what end? He'd made it clear there would never be anything between them. And that was probably for the best, because how could she trust anyone to stay, when everyone had abandoned her when she'd needed them most?

Before dark, Ace took Bear for a walk to the west end of his property since he needed to work off his frustration and check the fence Hudson had mentioned to him. Today hadn't gone exactly like he'd hoped. The minute their picnic ended, Jolene was off to help someone else. That's all they were to her, another stop on her do-gooder train.

But the way she looked at him made him believe for the briefest of moments that she was interested in him. Even the way she spoke made him think she wanted more, but she couldn't. Not with him. He'd been stupid to think otherwise.

Bear growled. A low, menacing tone of warning. Ace stopped and looked around. "What is it, boy?"

Not a sound around except an occasional chirp or chatter from nature. Bear crouched by his side, warning Ace something hid in the distance.

After a few moments, Bear settled back into

a more relaxed state. Probably just a noise Ace couldn't even hear. "What do you think, Bear?"

Bear looked up at him.

"You like her, that's obvious. But could two old broken bachelors like us ever keep a girl like Jolene happy? I can't even make it through a meal without having a meltdown."

They hiked up the hill, his stump rubbing against his prosthetic again, but at least he was able to keep going without stumbling or falling. Progress. "We owe Jolene our gratitude. Thanks to her, we can actually make this walk, huh?"

Bear looked up at him as if to agree.

"Maybe we could take her hiking. She said she likes to walk. That could be a great hobby if I can get moving even better."

Bear barked and growled and hunched.

Crunching leaves warned that something approached. "What's there, boy?" Ace chastised himself for not bringing the leash, but he was on his own property. And Bear never disobeyed a command. His former officer had trained him well.

"Who's there?" Ace called out, hoping some farmhand who was squatting on his land for a time would come out. He wouldn't care about that. He'd even pull a Jolene and offer him a meal.

No one responded, but Bear barked louder and his hackles rose. Ace hoped it wasn't a mountain lion because Bear would be injured if not killed. "Stay."

Ace held his breath and took a step back, easing away; hopefully, he could get a hold of Bear and get him home.

But a figure burst out of the bushes and stormed toward him. Bear lunged and attacked, his snout planted in the man's face, drooling and snapping at him.

Ace approached and discovered his neighbor, Benjamin. "What are you doing on my property?" Ace spotted the shotgun on the ground so he retrieved it. "Hunting on my land again, apparently."

"Get 'em off me," he shouted, his hands squeezing Bear's neck in a vain attempt to hold him off. But despite Benjamin's fear, it appeared that Bear only barked. He didn't bite, showing that the dog really wasn't a threat to anyone. If he still believed in God, he'd send up a big thank-you for that. No black marks on Bear's record.

Ace crouched down and said, "Sit," and held up a treat. Bear didn't bother getting off Benjamin, remaining seated on his stomach.

The man shimmied and scurried out from

under Bear as Ace lured him with the treat, but once he gobbled down the biscuit, he turned and growled at the man. Benjamin stood and backed away. "Get off my land," Ace yelled at him.

"All the deer are on this side, and a man's gotta eat."

Ace stood and towered over his neighbor. "You don't even eat it. You sell it instead of working your own land. Half the time, you leave them behind on my land, not even dressed. It's a waste, and I won't allow it. There is never a reason to kill something for sport or to only take part of it for financial gain."

"Well, I won't allow a dog to attack me. I'll have him put down."

Ace's hackles raised more than Bear's ever did. "You'll do no such thing."

The man took off running.

Not good. Ace didn't trust Benjamin. He'd exaggerate the story. "Come on, boy. We need to get home." With shotgun in hand, he headed back to his house with Bear trot-hopping by his side. By the time he reached the front door, police lights were twirling up his driveway. He hurried Bear inside to the new bed Ace had bought him. "Stay, and don't make a noise. Got it?"

Bear obeyed and he headed outside to keep

the police from coming anywhere close to him. Ace's pulse thundered; he didn't like this at all, but he needed to deal with it.

An officer got out of his vehicle and walked forward. "Are you Ace Gatlin?"

"Yes, sir." He made sure to keep his shoulders low and his hands relaxed. "What can I do for you, sir?"

"A neighbor claimed you attacked him and commanded your dog to bite him."

Ace shook his head. "I'm afraid you've been given false facts, Officer. The neighbor you speak of was on my property hunting deer. He kills them and takes what he can sell but leaves the rest. I believe he cut my fence. He was armed and attacked me."

"He held you at gunpoint?"

"Not exactly. He dropped the gun and ran with a threat to call the police on me."

The officer adjusted his belt and scanned the front of Ace's house. "Then you did attack him?"

"No, sir. As I mentioned, he came at me on my land." Ace took a breath to keep his temper under control. No need to give the officer reason to doubt him.

A van with Animal Control written on the side came down his drive and parked.

"And the dog?"

"I don't own a dog," Ace said. He didn't like to lie, but it was technically true that he didn't own a dog. Bear was here temporarily until he could be rehomed. Although, he'd considered a change of mind recently.

"Woof. Woof. Woof."

Talk about bad timing.

"No dog?" The officer turned to speak to the animal control man. Ace panicked and returned to the house, locking the door behind him. No way he'd let them take Bear and put him down. He wouldn't fail the dog like he'd failed his men. And he wouldn't be the one to tell Jolene that Bear was euthanized because Ace had him off leash.

The thought of any harm coming to Bear—an innocent, protective friend in his life—gutted him. Despite his attempts not to, he'd grown to care for the animal.

He slid his phone from his pocket; he had no idea what to do so he texted Jolene. If anyone could talk their way out of this, it was her. Police are here. Neighbor lied and they want animal control to take Bear.

Three dots danced in only seconds.

On my way.

If she was at the hospital, it could take ten to fifteen minutes for her to get there. What would he do to keep the police out for that long? He didn't care if they carted him off to jail, he wouldn't let them inside. He wouldn't fail Bear or Jolene like that.

"Mr. Gatlin, can you come out, please?" the officer called out. "We need to speak. If not, I'll have to call backup. The man claims that you have his gun, so if we have to come inside, someone could get hurt."

That wasn't good. If an enemy combatant was suspected of being armed, you terminated without prejudice. The best thing he could do was be unarmed. He grabbed the rifle, opened the window on the side of the house, tossed it outside, then went back to the living room. "I'm unarmed. Threw the weapon out the window. You'll find it on the side of the house."

"Mr. Gatlin, there's no reason for you to lock yourself inside. As I mentioned, I'm here for a conversation, that's all."

The officer banged on the door. The way his men had hammered on that door. But unlike his men, the officer didn't face an RPG on the other side.

Dizziness took hold and he collapsed on the couch, head between his legs. Nausea hit like a tsunami. He rocked to keep himself from screaming.

"Sir?"

"Go away," Ace ordered. Bear barked and came to his side.

Sounds. Rapid gunfire, explosion, screams.

Ace covered his ears and cried out, trying to keep it from taking control of him. It had been a year since he'd had an episode this bad. "It's not real. It's not real." But it was real. The explosion. The killing.

He didn't know how long he'd been lost in his terror, but a soft voice came through the door. "Ace, it's me. Can you open the door?"

"I won't let them take him. I won't fail again," he cried out, his voice strained to reach for help, a lifeline.

"We can't fix this unless you open the door." Jolene's voice carried a sweet caress that drew him enough out of his darkness to process. He managed to turn the lock but took up guard over Bear. His hands shook, his legs trembled, sweat poured down his back, the sounds still hammered in his head. Jolene placed her palm to his chest. "Breathe in."

He did as she told him.

"Out." She puckered her lips and blew out with him. "Again."

Bear raced by him. Ace lunged, but the officer squatted. "It's you."

The officer and Bear rolled around and hugged like they were lifelong friends.

Jolene slid her fingers between his. "You okay?"

He nodded but kept his eyes on Bear.

"You took Bear in? That's amazing. Last I heard, they were going to put him down. Thank you. Thank you so much." The officer's voice cracked. "He was my buddy's K-9. I wanted to take him, but the department said negative due to us having a three-month-old at home."

All the muscles in Ace's body relaxed at once, and he almost collapsed, but Jolene was there at his side. "Let's sit." She guided him to the couch and lowered him, then left, only to return a minute later with a damp cloth. With a light touch, she dabbed at his forehead and the back of his neck. "Everything's okay now."

"Listen, if what you say is true about your neighbor, he'll be the one facing a fine." The officer stood. "Don't know what's going on, but do you need an ambulance?"

Ace shook his head. "What about Bear?"

"Ms. Jolene here showed me the paperwork and explained what's going on. If the dog didn't bite your neighbor and he was trespassing in the attempt of illegally hunting, then I have a feeling he's going to withdraw his complaint and we can all forget this happened. But do us both a favor and keep Bear on a leash at all times outside."

"Yes, Officer. I promise." Ace managed to find the words to speak.

The door clicked shut and Jolene took his face in her soft hands. "You're a hero." She pressed a kiss to his cheek and all the darkness evaporated.

"I'm no hero." He wasn't; the word was bitter on his tongue. "I didn't do anything."

"You were willing to go to jail to protect Bear. I think you're a hero."

"I'm anything but that. Trust me." He leaned back on the couch and thought he'd pass out right then and there, but he eyed Jolene. "You're the amazing one. You remained calm and fixed the situation. You're one special lady. You know that, right?"

"I'm working on it. But I'm hoping to help someone else to see that about himself, too."

"Woof."

"You're special, too." Jolene laughed. A light sound that warmed the entire room.

In that moment, all Ace could think about was pulling Jolene into his arms and telling her how he really felt about her. Kissing her and showering her with all the attention she deserved but never asked for in her life. But he couldn't. Not until he could figure out how to deal with life and his guilt. Maybe someday he'd be worthy, but today wasn't that day.

Chapter Six

Jolene stood in front of the schedule board in the barn. Sunday flew by between church, women's Bible study, helping in the children's program and then working on the week's schedule. For some reason, her arm felt heavy writing on the board. Usually, she loved to plan and execute a week. But all she wanted to do was go check on Ace and Bear.

Juniper came into the barn with a box of new equipment she'd purchased. "You look tired. Maybe you should snag a nap."

"No, it's fine. I've got a lot to do before tomorrow. Charts to finish and schedule, and I'll need to be at the hospital before visiting hours end."

A soft sigh sounded, so Jolene capped her marker and turned to face Juniper. "What is it?"

"A nurse from the hospital called. They had the old home line number from when Hudson's grandmother went there. She wanted to get a message to you." Juniper set the box down and faced Jolene. "I'm afraid that the woman you were reading to each night passed away this morning peacefully."

"Oh." Jolene uncapped the marker, eyed the calendar on her phone and wrote the next appointment on the board.

"You okay?"

"Yeah. I'm glad God took her home. She wasn't living anymore." How many times had she begged God to release her from her own body while stuck in a hospital bed? But in this case, God listened to her prayers. The woman was old and was never going to get better. She closed her eyes and said a silent prayer before returning to work.

"Okay, well, why don't you relax tonight? You're welcome to join us for dinner, of course, or you can just rest in the apartment if you want some quiet time."

"No. I don't need quiet time." She hated the quiet; she even slept with a radio on most nights. "But I do have some things to take care of, so I won't be at dinner, if that's okay."

"Yes. You know you can join us whenever you want, though."

Jolene finished up the schedule and thought she'd try something new tonight. Instead of texting the hospital, Mindi and the retirement facility to see if anyone needed anything, she'd go check on Ace and Bear. She sent him a message to see if she could stop by.

He didn't answer, so she thought he was shut down after the incident last night. Should she go over anyway or give him more space? She eyed the flowers on her desk and remembered how adorable he was when he'd given them to her. There was something there but she couldn't force it so she decided to finish her charting. When she was halfway done with her work, her phone dinged.

Yes. Sorry. We were out in the fields finishing up for the day. I'll be ready in twenty if you want to come for dinner.

She held the phone to her chest and closed her eyes. "God, please open his heart. I know You can work miracles. I don't know that I'm the one to help him, but I'm trying. Please give me guidance."

With her oversize purse that she used on Sundays to house her Bible, she headed to the Gatlin farm. Lightning streaked across the sky and thunder rumbled through the land. Rain pelted her window but Ace ran out with an umbrella to get her. "That came out of nowhere."

"It was forecasted," Ace teased with a brow

waggle. "I guess you don't check the weather much."

"No. Not on weekends anyway since I'm not working with clients. After church and Bible study, it's all about paperwork."

He tucked her into his side. He smelled of fresh fall and cinnamon. Her favorite scents on earth.

Inside, she discovered where the cinnamon aroma came from in the form of food already set out in the kitchen. A turkey, mashed potatoes, a red candy-looking dish that smelled like cinnamon apples and bread with the rich smell of pumpkins. "What's all this?"

"I thought you'd enjoy a proper fall meal. When I was growing up, my grandmother would cook all this on the first fall day of the year. Most people had big Thanksgiving or Christmas dinners, but she liked to cook at the start of the season to welcome everyone to our home before the holidays made people too busy to enjoy a friendly meal. The candied apples are a family recipe passed down through generations of farmers. Simple but delicious."

"I can't wait to dig in." She looked around. "Where's Bear?"

Ace chuckled. It was light and fun and endearing, and she wished he'd do it more often. "He's pouting."

She sat down in the chair. "Why?"

"Because after he chased a duck into the pond and muddied himself, I made him take a bath. He apparently didn't like the soap. The only dog shampoo I could find at the store was too girlie for him. I think he's offended."

She laughed and he poured her some water, then sat across from her, so she folded her hands in front of her to pray. He dug into the potatoes and plopped some onto her plate but then set it down and followed her lead. But he didn't close his eyes or bow his head. Instead, he sat silently looking at her, so she said aloud, "Dear Heavenly Father, thank You for all of the gifts You've given us. The delicious food on the table, the gift of companionship with Bear and friendship. May Ms. Franklin rest in peace, and I pray that Your mercy is granted to those in need this night. Amen."

"Amen." Ace retrieved her plate once more and put a slab of meat, a spoonful of candied apples and a slice of pumpkin bread along with the potatoes.

"Wow, you must've been cooking all day." She took the plate and inhaled the hearty aroma of pepper, pumpkin and possibilities.

He shook his head. "Not really. Well, the turkey I started a few hours ago and I'd planned on just having that the next few days, but when you called I decided to add the side dishes and enjoy a real meal sitting down instead of in the living room watching the news with Bear drooling at my feet eyeing my every bite. This is much better."

She sliced a piece of meat and ate it. Buttery, melt-in-your-mouth turkey with a hint of sage exploded on her tongue. "Wow, did Bear get any of this?" She pointed her fork at her plate.

"No, he'll have to stop pouting first. The shampoo smell isn't that bad." He looked to the doorway. "Hey, Bear," he called out to the other room but Bear didn't respond.

She took a bite of her mashed potatoes and savored the salty goodness. "Wow, you really do know how to cook. Did your mother teach you?"

"No." He took a bite, chewed, then looked at her as if assessing whether he should share or not. She was thankful when he did. "My grandmother and grandfather raised me. Father died during a skirmish in the Middle East while my mother was pregnant with me. She passed away a few years later when she was hit by a drunk driver."

"I'm so sorry." She reached across the table and took his hand, squeezing it to let him know she was there for him.

"Don't be. I had an amazing life with my grandparents. My grandmother taught me to cook, and my grandfather showed me how to whittle. We'd sit on the front porch and carve what we'd see outside. They were good to me."

"Whittling? That sounds interesting."

"I can show you how. Perhaps a potential hobby to try?"

"Maybe." She shrugged, knowing she had no time for hobbies. "Are your grandparents still around?"

"No. They passed away about three years ago. I came back here after I was injured, but they both were sickly by then. My grandfather passed away a day after my grandmother because he said he couldn't live without her. They both died in their sleep peacefully. Honestly, I have nothing to complain about as far as childhood goes. Mine was pretty perfect."

"That's good," she said and returned to eating.

"What about you? Are your folks still around?"

"Around?" She took a sip of water to try to choke down her resentment. "No. Alive, yes."

He blinked at her and set his fork down. She

tried to ignore him and keep eating but after a few bites, she realized he wasn't going to stop staring at her until she shared. "My parents have always been busy traveling, working, that kind of thing. I was an only child raised by nannies and such. I have nothing to complain about either. There was always money and I never had to struggle when I was young."

"But?" Ace quirked a brow.

"No *but*. It's the truth." She reached for her fork but it was his turn to cover her hand.

"You were lonely," he said in a tone that soothed her nerves. "You mentioned the fact you were taken care of by nannies twice now. I deduce that meant you were left alone a lot by your parents."

She sighed and bit her bottom lip, willing no tears to appear, but that lump in her throat that always rose when she thought about her family was stubborn. "I was."

"You said that you wouldn't want anyone to feel as alone as you did when you were in the hospital. They weren't with you?" His fingers tightened around her hand and his brow furrowed.

"No. Well, they flew home for a few weeks and Mom cried in front of doctors and nurses, but from what I understand, the minute they put the trach in, she left, and Dad didn't even make it that long." With her free hand, she touched her neck where the scar remained as evidence of her captivity.

He moved his chair closer and slid his plate around the table. "Were you in an accident?"

"No. It was worse." She swallowed and pushed through the memories. "Long story short... I got a flu shot when I was younger. It was back when they used live vaccines, and I developed what's called Guillain-Barré syndrome from it. I had a severe case and lost the ability to move anything, even breathe on my own, but I was awake, unable to speak in the silence of my room. My parents removed me from the hospital and gave me private care, which was worse. They came in, changed linens, tended to my needs and then left. I could hear but no one spoke to me. I was alone."

"Except for God," Ace said in a gravelly tone. "That's why you work so hard at the hospital reading to people and volunteering around town. You don't want anyone to ever feel like that."

"No, I don't." She took in a shuttered breath. "But it wasn't all bad. It's funny."

"What is?" He tucked her hair behind her ear, his touch soothing the stinging fear on her skin.

"You can hear God so clearly and feel Him when you're silent. Most people are too busy talking to listen or caught up in themselves to hear." She shrugged. "And in the end, to my parents' horror, I understood that my softball scholarship and ambitions were not what was truly important in life. Helping people through a difficult time was my calling. I found it to be a gift to know exactly what I wanted out of life when I escaped my tomb."

"You've been through so much. I wish I could've been there for you." He raked his finger down her trach scar. "I would never abandon you."

That was easy to say, but no one would've stuck around that long. She sniffled, fighting to maintain control. Tears didn't help solve anything; that she learned a long time ago. "No, I don't think you would have. The illness lasted too long for my friends or dates or family. By the time I regained the ability to breathe on my own, walk and dress myself, no one was left. It was as if I'd been dropped into my life seventeen years into it. My softball scholarship was gone, which meant I had to use my parents' money, which was humbling for me."

He slid his thumb along her jawline to her chin. How many times had she craved physical touch when she was in sensory isolation because no one cared to be close to her?

He smiled, that mischievous, full-of-tenderness grin that made his scar stretch into a thin line. "I don't know. I'm pretty stubborn and I'm like fleas. Hard to get rid of at times."

That brought a smile from deep inside. "That you are. Stubborn, I mean." And for the first time in her life, she dared to believe someone might actually stick around and be there with her no matter what. "What I went through isn't like going to war, though."

"No, but there are all kinds of battles we have to face in life."

How could he not belittle her trauma? Her own parents had told her to let it go a month after she'd recovered, telling her that dwelling in the past never helped anyone. They hadn't been wrong, but a little validation sometimes goes a long way. And Ace was the first person to ever validate her feelings.

She turned to face him, resting both hands on his knees. "Tell me. Please. Not because I'm a therapist or a friend, but because I care and I want to know more about you."

He looked away. "Then you'll want to leave."

"Then you don't know me at all. Nothing you

can say will make me leave. It was war. Bad things happened."

He slid back, slumping in his chair. "How can you stay when God wouldn't even stick around?"

She knew better than that, but making him see He never left would be a challenge and it would be up to God to help his heart heal. "You know I don't believe that, but you can try to change my mind."

He eyed the cabinet in the corner she'd opened that day. The only place in the house with a cobweb inside. After several seconds, he stood, went to the cabinet and brought back several envelopes and pictures. "These were my men. Only two of us survived. Myself and the man who wrote these letters."

She eyed the sealed envelopes. "You haven't opened them."

He shook his head and she noticed his breath coming a little faster and shorter, but she nudged further. "Why?"

"Because I can't face what I already know. It was my fault these men died, and this one..." He pointed to a man with shaggy blondish hair about an inch shorter than him but with a similar build. "He came back a double amputee."

The way his gaze dropped told her his grief

and guilt weighed heavy on him. "You don't know what he has to say if you've never opened the letters." She nudged them toward him, but he pushed them aside.

"Not tonight. When I'm ready."

She nodded. "I can respect that. Let's finish this amazing meal."

They settled in side by side and enjoyed their meal. Ace offered her more, but she sat back and rubbed her belly. "I can't fit another bite, but it was so delicious. You're spoiling me."

"Good, you deserve to be spoiled. About time someone looked after you for a change." Ace took her dish, but she stood and went to the sink.

"No way. You cooked, I'll clean." She slid on the gloves resting on the side of the sink. "Hey, Bear, you want to clean my plate?" she hollered out of the kitchen.

He stuck his nose around the cabinet, then nudged into the room in a bad-dog hobble. Fresh roses filled the room. "Oh no, it is that bad," she whispered to Ace.

"I know, but don't tell him. Hopefully, it'll fade by tomorrow. It was brackish mud or roses."

"Here, boy. You can have a double portion for being so good." Bear lifted his head and licked her hand.

"How about you wash and I dry. Never put

in a dishwasher." Ace picked up a towel and held out his hand.

She passed him a dish; he wiped it dry and set it in the cabinet. They fell into a rhythm like a family. A real family. Dog at her feet snoring, him at her side, a full belly and a warm, peaceful home. A foreign concept that she wanted to embrace and hold on to tightly. But how could she hold on to someone who always wanted to push everyone away?

She sighed and removed her gloves, resting them on the counter.

"What are you smiling about?" Ace shoulder-bumped her.

"Nothing." She waved him off. "It's silly."

"I want to know. Tell me." Ace folded the towel and set it with even ends over the handle of the stove, then turned to face her.

"Just reflecting on the fact that I've never done this."

He stiffened the way he did when he thought he'd done something wrong. "What?"

"Relax." She stepped closer to him. "I'm talking about doing dishes."

His head tilted. "You've never done dishes before? You really were a spoiled rich girl."

She gave him her best stern expression with a hip pop for extra measure.

He held his hands up to his shoulders. "Kidding."

Bear yawned and stretched.

"My family didn't do things together that didn't involve a hotel room and some fancy dinner or staff that did the work." With a hesitant step, she moved closer to him. "To me, it feels so much like a real family. It sounds silly, but you have a nice home, and with Bear and you..." She looked up at him to find his eyes wide and his breath short so she stepped away. Her stomach knotted. "Don't worry, I know you're not the relationship type. You've been clear about that, and I appreciate that more than you know. I just enjoyed the moment. A hint at what life could offer someday... Maybe."

Ace fought to find his breath, to move, to speak. Frozen not by fear for the first time but hope. But did he dare to believe he could become a different man? He wanted to pull her into his arms and promise her dishes and dogs and delicious food every night for the rest of her life, but he couldn't. He eyed the letters taunting him on the kitchen table. He needed to do something before he could ever move on, something he'd never wanted to do before. But could he face his past to have a possible future with someone like Jolene?

He didn't deserve it, but she did, and he'd spend his life taking care of her the way she deserved and would never abandon her.

When she left him standing with mouth open in the kitchen, he knew she wouldn't leave without saying goodbye, so he stalled by making some hot chocolate to regain his composure and retrieved a piece of wood and a carving knife from the workshop in the garage. He slid the small piece of wood and sheathed carving knife into his pocket and headed to find Jolene outside on the front porch swing.

Rain plinked the tin roof like the background of a sweet country song. She looked radiant in the moonlight. From her blond hair to her leggings. Perfect. That's what she was. "You really handled things well yesterday with the police. How did you become so calm and able to deal with people so well?"

"I had some training." She winked and took the hot chocolate from him.

He sat down next to her. "Thought you were full."

"There is always room for chocolate of any kind." She stirred the whipped cream into the dark liquid.

He took a sip of his hot chocolate, then abandoned it to the side and retrieved the wood and knife. "Thought we could try it."

She blinked at him with a sideways, are-you-crazy glance. "Didn't you tell me I wasn't good at chopping vegetables? Now you want me to whittle wood?"

He shrugged. "I'll make you a deal. You try some new hobbies, and I'll try to face my past."

She pressed her lips together. "Another challenge. I'll take it. Hand me the wood."

"Whoa, now. Not so fast. I do want you to keep your fingers," he teased but handed it over. "Just make sure to slice away from you." He winked. "You're going to do what is called a push cut, like this." He took her left hand and positioned it to hold the wood in a way that she would hopefully not slice her finger off, and then held her right hand with the knife in it to guide her cut.

Her soft skin distracted him, but he forced his attention to remain on safety. He guided her hand to slide away from her until she took a chunk of wood off.

"Hey, I did it." She smiled, her perfect white teeth making a breath-catching appearance. "Let me try on my own."

To his disappointment, she shrugged his hand

away and did it on her own. She didn't stop, slice after slice, then held it up. "Ah, I think I made a toothpick for a giant."

He shrugged. "It takes practice."

The evening air must've been too chilly because she shivered at his side. He took the knife and wood from her and set it aside. "We'll do more later. Drink up for now." He retrieved his hot chocolate, which was lukewarm now, put his free arm around her and pulled her against him to stave off the cold. That's what he told himself anyway.

She sat rod straight for a moment but then settled into his side, even leaning into him. A woman had never fit so perfectly in his arms, his side, his life. He sipped his drink to keep himself from doing something stupid like kissing her. That would be the worst thing he could do right now. She deserved better than a broken man who'd only let her down. He had work to do before he opened up to any possibilities with someone as special as Jolene.

Bear joined them and plopped down at the top of the steps as if keeping watch to protect them.

They sat listening to the rain, rocking and cuddling until he noticed her cup lower further and further into her lap. He set his to the side and slipped hers from her hands before she spilled it on herself.

Deep breathing told him she'd dozed off. Good, she needed the rest. He set her cup with his, ran his fingers through her soft hair and pressed a kiss to the top of her head.

Bear shot up as if to tell him he needed to keep his space from her but then came over and put his chin on her lap, stirring her awake. She stretched in Ace's arms and then sat up. "Sorry, how long was I out?"

"Only moments. Go back to sleep."

She sat up. "Some friend I am. You make a lovely meal and I fall asleep on you." With a flick of her wrist, she stood. "I better get going anyway. I have to finish charting before the morning."

"You do too much." He shook his head because he knew she wouldn't listen. "I understand why you do it now, but you can't be everything to everyone. Even God took a rest day."

She went inside and grabbed her large bag and shook her head free of sleep. "I know that but this is my job. My calling." With an awkward pause, she remained still as if waiting for him to do something. Eventually, she held out her hand and said, "Thanks, friend, see you tomorrow."

"Maybe we can try whittling again."

"Sorry, don't think that's for me."

"Then we'll try something else. Remember our deal." He held her hand and wanted to pull her close, but he had something he needed to do tonight. After he faced his past, tomorrow he could look to the future. "Good night, Jolene."

"Good night." And in only a moment, she was gone from his world, leaving a hint of loneliness in her wake. Something he hadn't felt in all the years he'd been alone. She'd changed him when he hadn't been looking.

Bear lumbered by, so Ace retrieved the mugs, headed to the kitchen and set them in the sink. He cringed at leaving dishes unwashed, but if he didn't rip open one of those envelopes immediately, he'd never do it. And if he wanted to get Jolene to concentrate on something besides work, and to be worthy of her, he needed to do this. With one yank and a tug of paper, he held the first message his former best friend had written and braced to face the condemnation and anger.

Ace,
I wish I knew why you ran off before I could get to you. I'm worried that you're not recovering, but the only address I had was your grandparents' so I hope this note

*gets to you. I need you. We lost our friends and we each suffered serious wounds. I hate that our unit, my family, is no longer together. Please write soon to let me know how you are. I'll be in the VA for another couple of weeks. If I don't hear from you by the time I'm discharged, then I'll write again.
Your best friend and comrade,
Logan Brock*

Ace choked on his own emotion bubbling up from deep inside him. No hate. No anger, only a plea for his friend to return. But he hadn't. He'd never gone back to check on Logan because he'd been sure he'd never want to see him again.

He collapsed into the chair and opened the next letter and found more of the same. Letter after letter contained pleas for him to come find Logan, to talk to him, to be there for him. Ace found the last letter with an email address listed and a phone number. This time it wasn't a plea, it was downright begging. The once fearless man Ace looked up to, despite Logan being a lower rank, begged him to reach out. But he hadn't. He'd abandoned Logan the way Jolene's parents had abandoned her.

Alone. His best friend had struggled with

employment and housing and Ace could've helped but he didn't because he was too much of a coward to face what he'd done to him. Ace crumbled the letters and for the first time since he'd woken in the hospital, he cried. Cried for his lost friends, those he'd failed, but more for the alive one he'd abandoned.

All night, he sat in front of his computer trying to craft the perfect email to Logan, but how could he explain why he'd never answered? By the time morning rolled around, he finally typed.

Logan,
I'm sorry I wasn't there for you. I'm sorry our friends died because I volunteered us for that mission. I hate myself and in punishing myself for what happened, I abandoned you. I'll send anything you need, but you never have to see me again.
Ace

At the first ray of light, Ace went to work barking at farmhands and slipping back into his grumpy ways, but he didn't care. Nothing mattered because he deserved nothing. He didn't stop to eat or rest. He didn't even think about returning to his big, empty house until the sun went down and he couldn't see to work any longer.

"Wages?" one of the hands called after him.

Ace waved them to follow because there was no way he'd make it to the barn to put them in the box. Limping, he managed to climb the stairs to the house to retrieve the checks, leaving the door open so he wouldn't have to get back up. He grabbed the checkbook and stumbled to the couch, where he quickly scribbled out payments.

Bear whined and sat by his side.

Ace removed his prosthetic and found the wrap bloodied. Good; he deserved it. He deserved everything God punished him with. He'd done worse than cause the death and injuries of his men. He'd done exactly what had caused Jolene so much pain: he'd abandoned his best friend, leaving him alone to face the world. He'd never felt so worthless and undeserving.

"What have you done?" Jolene's voice shrieked from the doorway, and she rushed over, falling to her knees in front of him. "Enough is enough. I'm going to speak and you're going to listen. Right after I clean up your mess."

Chapter Seven

Blood dotted the cloth around his stump. Jolene's chest stung at the sight. She went to the bathroom, got a washcloth and searched through his cabinet for some ointment, buying some time to compose herself before she started yelling at him for being so careless with his health.

Why wouldn't he get a new prosthetic? Enough was enough. She would drive him to the hospital herself for an evaluation if that's what it took.

She returned to the living room as some of the farmhands filtered out of the house looking a little more worn out than normal. When the last one walked out, she shut the front door, locked it and knelt in front of Ace.

"I think I'm in trouble, Bear."

He skittered to his bed.

"Thanks for the backup," Ace called after him.

"Not funny," she snipped.

"Kind of funny." He reached for the cloth, but

she shook her head and peeled back the compression liner, eliciting a hiss. His face bleached white. "Serves you right. What were you thinking?"

The liner wasn't even a good-quality one, more of a typical sock. Who gave this to him? Knowing Ace, he probably bought something on his own instead of using anything his therapist ordered for him.

"You don't need to do that." He scooted farther back on the couch and tried to move his leg away from her, but she glowered at him.

"Don't even think about it." Beyond sweat, there wasn't an odor except the metallic smell of blood, so that was a good sign. That and no oozing meant he didn't have an active infection.

"You don't want to see my stump, it's not pretty."

"I'm a therapist who started her career in a burn center. Trust me, this won't shock me so get over yourself."

He nodded and sat back but gripped a pillow tight to his chest.

She knew this would make him feel vulnerable, but at the moment she didn't care about his feelings, she only cared about helping. "How'd you let it get this bad? Why didn't you tell me about this last night?" She managed to remove the last of his barrier and eyed the chaffing marks along the edge and down the side of his knee.

"Wasn't there last night," he said in a guttural tone.

"This is too much for a few extra hours of work in a day." She took the damp cloth and dabbed at the puckered skin.

"Define *a few extra hours*," he chuckled.

"Seriously? You think this is funny? You risk infection, needing restorative surgery, losing more of your leg. Did your therapist not go over the risks and instruct you on the importance of healthy skin?" She uncapped the disinfectant and poured it over his wound, eliciting another hiss.

His fingers dug into the pillow and he closed his eyes while bubbles formed on the open edges of the wound. "I think you're enjoying this."

"I think you're ridiculous. How many extra hours?"

"Can't talk, stings too much."

She blew on his knee until the bubbles settled, then dabbed with the cloth to dry it well.

He watched her, his mouth ajar and gaze locked on her. It had to be hard for him to let her see his wounds, to be exposed to her like this. She wasn't sure what made her do it, but she leaned in and pressed a kiss to his knee.

"It's ugly," he ground out, but his eyes didn't leave her.

"No. It's beautiful because you survived."

"No. It's a reminder of what I lost. Not just me but my men. They died because of me."

"You keep saying that but why do you blame yourself? Maybe if you stopped grunting and started talking, you'd figure some things out in your life." She squirted ointment on her finger and dabbed it along the worst of the damage.

"Because I volunteered us for the mission," he blurted. He rested his head back on the couch, ran a hand through his hair and rubbed his temples. "I wanted to prove myself. The mission commander tried to send the other team in but they were one man down. Since we were at full strength, it made sense for us to go. Only the intel was bad. A trap. An RPG fired through the door and blasted us all, killing three of my men and wounding my best friend and me." His words gushed out along with his breath.

She sat back on her heels. "Where is your best friend now?"

He eyed the kitchen. "Not doing well. I didn't just fail him once. I keep failing him. You see? I'm not the man you want me to be. You think I'm some sort of hero who served his country, but I'm not."

"The letters. They were from your friend and you opened them, didn't you?" She knew there had to be a trigger, something to cause him to punish himself like this.

"Yeah, I did. But it wasn't what I thought it was. I'd spent years thinking he'd sent me those letters to tell me he hated me, that he blamed me. I was too much of a coward to read them, but that's not what he wrote. He wrote to tell me he needed me, and I never read them. Time and time again, I've failed him. I told you I would never abandon you like your parents, but that's what I did to him. I was wrong." He picked at a cushion thread. "I'd fail you too if you let me into your life."

"You're right." She gathered her supplies and stood. "I don't want to be with a man who causes himself harm because he's not ready to face the truth of his actions. Get your act together. Tomorrow, I'm making a call to get you in to see someone about a new fitting, or you can call the VA. Either way, I'm not going to let you live like this anymore."

"You can't force me, you know."

"Oh, I can when I take that leg and turn it into a chew toy for Bear."

Bear groaned from the corner but didn't move.

"That's not very therapeutic of you."

"Good thing I'm not your therapist." She returned the supplies to the bathroom, then came out and plopped down on the couch next to him. Her anger simmered and mixed with the anxiety of her day. "I was looking forward to coming over to spend time with you and Bear tonight. My day was tough and I just wanted to see my friend, but then I get here to this?" She studied the button of his shirt. Her emotions swirled into a puddle of worry and exhaustion.

He tipped her chin up to look at him. "Hey, I'm sorry. Why don't you tell me about your day."

She wanted to fall into his arms and be held and kissed and protected from the world, but she couldn't trust he'd be here tomorrow. "Grant was rejected."

"The one you worked on last week?" he asked.

She nodded. "And Jimmy, a little boy I'm working with, had to go in for another surgery after a fall at home. It's going to set him back months. The poor little guy worked so hard to make progress and now it's all gone." *God give me strength.*

"Let me clean up, and I'll come right back and we can talk through everything."

"You're not going up those stairs right now. I'll get you a change of clothes and a towel and you can use this bathroom." She bolted off the couch and went to his bedroom, ignoring his protests.

It didn't take long to find a change of clothes since his drawers were organized with everything rolled and placed in rows that matched in height and width.

She returned and dropped everything into the bathroom. Before she could exit, he stood on his one leg, holding the doorframe.

"I can manage from here."

"Door stays unlocked in case you fall."

"Yes, ma'am."

He closed the door and she sat on the floor by Bear, petting him, rolling through her thoughts of how to handle Ace Gatlin and her growing feelings for a man who was too broken to open his heart to anyone.

A little while later, he came out with the towel draped around his neck. He stood in flannel pajama bottoms with the leg tied under his one knee and a long-sleeve shirt with three buttons at the top snug across his broad chest. A picture-perfect Christmas catalog for clothing with a beautiful, broad-shouldered, one-legged model.

She sat on the couch and tapped the cushion at her side. After discarding his towel, he hopped to the couch to join her. He slid his arm around her, and his fresh woodsy aroma invited her closer, but she pressed her hand to his side to keep from falling into him.

"Please, tell me what you plan to do about this. I thought we were getting past you torturing yourself. I can't sit back and watch you do this day after day."

He looked to the fireplace as if answers rested in the shadows. "I sent an email to him, apologizing, but I haven't checked to see if he's responded."

A part of her relaxed. "That's good."

He tugged her toward him, but when she didn't move, he sighed. "And I'll call the VA tomorrow about a new prosthesis. Okay?"

With that, he opened his arms to her, and without hesitation, she sank into his embrace, cradled in a cocoon of warmth and strength. The thu-thump of his heart eased her anxiety.

"I'm sorry I added to your day." His lips pressed to the top of her head, sending warmth down her neck. A man so powerful and stubborn yet sensitive and soft. She'd never guessed someone like him lived in this world. If only he could see his gifts instead of his flaws.

"Can I fix you something to eat?" he offered.

"You're not getting off this couch, mister." She wagged her finger at him but didn't move to face him. Too tired, too worn out to make the effort.

He brushed her hair away from her face and pressed another kiss to her head. "What can I do to help make your day better?"

The feeling of physical contact with someone when she felt alone made her almost believe he'd never abandon her. "Hold me for a while?"

He tucked her in tight against him.

"I'm proud of you for opening those letters and reading them." She wanted him to know that he'd done something good, made a step toward healing. Wanted to encourage him to keep going and grow.

"Thanks. We'll see if he responds. If so, I want to know what I can do to help him, if it isn't too late."

"He'll reach out." She rested her ear on his chest and savored his strong heartbeat.

"Why do you think that?"

"Because God works that way."

He chuckled. "Not sure He'd want to work in my mess. But I'm glad you believe that. And I'm glad God was there when you needed Him most."

"Listen, there was a reason you opened those letters now. Maybe your friend is doing better and you're the one that needs him. Who knows why. I just know He's working in our lives every day."

"Thanks for coming over and hanging out with us tonight when I'm sure all you wanted to do was to finish your work and get some sleep."

"I wanted to see you more." She looked up at him and his strong lips. Every ounce of her wanted to kiss him, but she knew he wasn't emotionally available. Not yet. And when they did kiss, she wanted to know he was all in with her.

Her phone buzzed, but instead of releasing her, he held her tighter. "Don't get that. Stay."

Almost every ounce of her wanted to remain in that spot, but she couldn't. What if someone needed her? She slid her phone from her pocket and saw the text. Yes, she was needed, so she hopped to her feet. "Sorry, got to go. One of my clients just texted that he's stuck in his car and can't get out. He had a hip replacement."

"Can I help?"

"No, I need you to stay here and not make that wound any worse. No working on the farm tomorrow. Keep that leg up and dry."

"Yes, ma'am." He saluted and went to stand but she shook her head. "I'll show myself out. Bear, you're in charge. Don't let him leave this house tomorrow, got it?"

"Woof."

"Thanks, at least I can count on one of you." She opened the door. "Call or text if you hear back from Logan."

"I'll be fine, and you already have too much to deal with to have me in your life." His voice sounded distant and broken.

She turned on her heels. "You're not my patient. I want to be here. And friends don't shut friends out."

"Fine, I promise not to shut you out if you promise me you won't be up all night working. You need to get some rest."

She shut the door because she didn't want to lie to him. Tonight would be an all-nighter. If she didn't find a new grant, things would be tight to keep the hippotherapy program running much beyond the year. Not that Hudson didn't have money to keep it afloat, but from what she understood it was tied up in a legal issue with his father. And she couldn't lose this job. Not when she'd finally found a place that felt like home. And people that made her feel like family.

For a few glorious minutes, Ace believed that Jolene would want to spend time with him and forget about the rest of the world. The way she'd cared for his wound with such tenderness, her lips pressed to his scars, jolted him into believing anything could be possible. That something between them truly grew. He thought about telling her how he really felt, but he'd been a fool. The second someone in need reached out, she was gone.

That's all he was, a stopover on her list of people to help. He told himself it didn't matter, but it did. He wanted more from Jolene than a friendship. She was part of the reason he'd put himself out there to email Logan. To do what she had asked and open his heart to try to grow and move past the pain. But it had backfired. First from learning that he'd let Logan down over and over again, and then discovering he was only a number in the long list of pity projects.

He wouldn't make that mistake again. "Come on, Bear, let's go to bed early. I've got things to take care of in the morning."

Unable to stomach putting his prosthesis back on, he had to hop to the stairs. Using his upper-body strength in conjunction with his one leg, he managed to make it up to bed. But to his disappointment, at 4:22 a.m. his nightmare returned with vengeance.

When he awoke on the floor in the corner,

he could smell the smoke and taste the grit of sand in his teeth. Real, all so real. Bear sat at the doorway as if waiting for him, but Ace saw in the way Bear held his head low that he'd suffered the same kind of night.

Unable to return to work with his stump still raw, he managed to get downstairs and start coffee, settle into his desk chair and open his laptop. To his fear and delight, an email from Logan had indeed arrived. With a deep breath for courage, he opened it.

Ace,
It's so good to hear from you. I don't know why you're apologizing when we all wanted the job, begged you to make it happen. Anyway, I'd love to speak with you. Right now, I'm living in a halfway house for veterans since no one wants to hire a double amputee with no college degree. Don't get me wrong, I've had a couple of jobs, but mostly seasonal. My wife left me after I lost the last job. She honestly couldn't handle my challenges, so I moved into here.
Call me.
Logan

Ace stared at his laptop and knew he had to do something. Could Jolene have been right? Did God somehow influence him to open those letters because now was the time he and Logan needed each other? If so, how could Ace not help his once best friend? He could hear the tone of desperation in his friend's email, so he hit Return and typed, I'll call you tomorrow. I have a farm and hire farmhands. If interested, let me know. Room and board would be included.

He hit Enter before he changed his mind. He had no desire to have a roommate or deal with another cranky wounded vet like himself, but how could he turn his back on his only remaining family? Maybe not in the traditional sense, but they'd become brothers through battle.

In only a matter of seconds, his email dinged, an oddly quick response considering the early morning hour, but that just told Ace that Logan probably struggled with sleep as much as any other veteran haunted by his service.

He read the message that Logan would love to come as soon as Ace would have him. This would please Jolene, show her that he could move past his own issues to help someone else with theirs. Not that it mattered. If anything, it would probably get her to move on if he healed so she could help the next person. Good. Then she wouldn't come around so much, confusing him into believing there were possibilities between them.

All day, he thought about God and Jolene and having a new person living with him. Bear moped around as if depressed, so Ace managed to get the ball and throw it for him, but Bear didn't chase it. Hopefully, Jolene would come by later and cheer him up.

The fall festival was only a few weeks away, so they needed to make sure Bear was ready for the final evaluation. According to Jolene, animal control still reported the visit to the farm, and they'd given Sheriff Monroe a deadline to send in her report to the state.

It was late, well after dinner, when Jolene's headlights shone through the front window. He finally managed to put on his prosthesis and make it to the front porch steps. She shuffled from her car not even looking up at him.

"Hey, you okay?" he called out to her, but she didn't answer.

"Jolene?" Something wasn't right. He stumbled down the steps and reached her a second before she collapsed into his arms. His pulse hammered. "What's wrong? Wake up."

He brushed her hair out of her eyes and discovered she was out cold. "Hang on." With his arm slid under her knees and his other behind her back, he managed to pick her up, and despite the pain shooting from his knee, he made it into the house, then lowered her onto the couch, ready to grab his phone to call 9-1-1.

Her eyes fluttered open. "What happened?"

His pulse calmed to a thudding against his neck. "What happened? You fainted."

She laughed. "I don't faint."

"You did, and I carried you inside. Are you sick? Should I take you to the hospital? Call an ambulance?" He pressed his hand to her forehead.

"No. No." She rubbed her eyes and sat up but swooned so he eased her back down.

"What's going on?"

"Nothing. I forgot to eat and I didn't get much sleep. I guess I'm just a little run-down."

"A little?" Anger chilled him. "Listen, you gave me a lecture yesterday about not overdoing it, and then you go and do this. Stay here and don't move."

"Where're you going?" she asked, snagging his hand.

"To get you some food, and then I'm tucking you in on this couch for a nice long nap. No argument."

She didn't give one because she leaned back and before her head even rested against the cushion, soft snores sounded through her parted lips. Something had to give. He'd speak to Hudson and Juniper and let them know this couldn't continue. That Jolene would end up sick if she kept up this pace. He'd go over and help and also he'd call the hospital and tell them she wouldn't be volunteering for a while, and the church, and anyone else who expected her to donate her time. He'd cover all her jobs if needed.

He heated up some leftovers but decided she needed to sleep, so he settled in to cradle her head in his lap, stroking her soft hair from her face. Beautiful and peaceful, she slept there for hours not budging. At one point, she rolled over but went right back to sleep. When she finally did wake up, he'd let her know this was going to stop. The way she'd ordered him to stop punishing himself, he was equally determined that she was going to stop avoiding her trauma.

Maybe if she trusted that someone would be there for her, she'd open her heart and heal from those who'd abandoned her. And if he had anything else to say about it, he'd tell her that he was a selfish man and despite all the other reasons, he really wanted her to give up some of her volunteer jobs so she'd have more time to spend with Bear and himself.

Hours passed, and despite the cramping in

Ace's hip and leg, he didn't move. Bear settled in by their side as if he couldn't be too far away. Poor guy was definitely struggling. If only he knew what to do for him. He hadn't chased his tail or the ball since the incident with Benjamin three days ago.

The old clock on the mantel chimed midnight and Jolene bolted up from the couch, spinning in all directions. Eyes wide, she searched the room. He knew that look. He'd seen it too often in his men and in the mirror.

It was terror.

"Hey, it's okay." He eased toward her like you would a wild animal.

"What? Where?" She pressed her palms to her forehead and spun until he caught her arms and settled her to look straight at him.

"I'm here. You're fine. You fell asleep on the couch at my place." Ace rubbed her arms and studied her vacant eyes until she blinked several times and her eyes finally focused on him.

"You didn't leave me alone?" Her words were shattered into bits that he had to decipher, but he did, and it crushed him.

"I'd never leave you."

She threw her arms around his neck and he held her tight, as tight as he could without hurting her, so she knew he'd never let her go. And he didn't want to. He wanted to hold her for the rest of his days, but that was dangerous because as much as she needed someone, that someone wasn't him. Besides, the second someone else needed her, she'd be gone. But in this moment, he was her person. The one to stave off the anguish and make her whole again. And he'd put her back together piece by piece because despite how he felt, she deserved to have someone look after her.

When she relaxed into his arms, he eased her back onto the couch, placed a quilt over her small frame, then sat on the floor by her side, easing her large purse out of the way. "You need rest and I vow not to leave you until you wake in the morning. Sleep."

"No, I should…" Her eyes fluttered. "Cooking."

He figured she'd already slipped into a dream world.

"Hobby, learn to cook. With you. I…"

Cooking? She wanted to do something with him beyond dog and human therapy? A light shone so bright inside him, he felt like it would illuminate the world.

In a matter of seconds, she faded. Exhaustion. Pure exhaustion, and the only cure was rest.

He sat by her side thinking about sitting next

to her on the couch watching cooking shows, working together in the kitchen and sitting at the table trying their creations.

Bear came over and nudged her purse until a black leather-bound book tumbled out, then he settled with his paw on it.

"What's that, boy?"

Ace flipped it over and saw *Holy Bible* written in gold embossment. His chest tightened. He studied Bear. No way; it had to be a coincidence. God couldn't reach him through a dog. Not even one as special as Bear.

With shaking hands, Ace lifted the heavy book. That's all it was, a book of writing by men. It didn't speak to him anymore. It hadn't for a long time. Yet, he put it on his lap and patted Bear and eyed Jolene.

He shook off the silly thought that God was reaching out to him. "Jolene reads the Bible to people at the hospital who can't move. Maybe if I read it to her, she'll relax and have a restful sleep and wake without panic."

The thought of being trapped in a body that didn't move, left alone in the world, sounded like more torture than anything he'd ever faced in war. For Jolene, he'd read from the Bible. "Where do I begin?" He looked at Bear, but he only rested his head on his paw as if he needed to listen, too.

Ace let the book fall open to where one of the ribbons marked a place and looked at the page in front of him.

> 1 John 4:16 *And we have known and believed the love that God hath to us. God is love; and he that dwelleth in love dwelleth in God, and God in him.*

As if God's words blasted more shrapnel from his heart, a once raw, fiery wound faded to a dull ache. He rubbed his chest, feeling the remnants of pain and the beginning of something new. He read it three more times to himself and once more aloud, each repetition chipping away at his defenses.

He looked to the ceiling as if he could see Heaven beyond the wood and plaster. "But God, You can't love me. I've made so many mistakes. Love?" One small word that carried such a heavy weight. "I'm not worthy of love."

The silence that followed was deafening, pressing in on him from all sides. He felt as if the walls were closing in, forcing him to confront the truth he had been running from for so long. His breath quickened, and his hands shook. He clutched his chest harder, as if trying to keep his heart from breaking apart.

But then, amid the turmoil, a warmth spread from his chest, radiating outward. It was subtle at first, like the first rays of dawn breaking through the night. The warmth grew stronger, chasing away the cold darkness that had long resided within him. Tears welled up in his eyes as he felt the immense weight of his past mistakes lift, replaced by an overwhelming sense of peace.

He remembered waking in the hospital and being cared for by a sweet nurse, but when Ace discovered the fate of his men, he had turned away from love, from grace and from hope. The memories flooded back—the refusal of therapy, shutting himself off from his one friend who'd survived—each one a testament to his failures and regrets. Yet, with each painful recollection, the warmth only grew, as if God's love was pouring into every crack and crevice of his shattered heart.

A whisper of a feeling swept over him like a soft hug of forgiveness...no, love. God loved him. It was a truth he had never allowed himself to believe, but now it resonated deep within him, unwavering and undeniable. Tears spilled over, running down his cheeks in a torrent of release.

"But God," he whispered again, his voice trembling, "how can You love someone like me?" The question hung in the air, but this time, it wasn't met with silence. It was met with an unspoken assurance, a divine presence that filled the room and wrapped around him like a comforting embrace.

In that moment, he felt something break within him, not with pain but with the joy of liberation. His heart, once encased in the armor of bitterness and disbelief, opened up to the possibility of love and redemption. He took a deep, shuddering breath, feeling lighter than he had in years.

A soft mewl sounded from Jolene, drawing his attention to the sweet, beautiful woman on his couch who gave the world so much love yet expected nothing in return. Was that the secret? To give others more of yourself to allow room for God in your heart? But could he dare to hope these words applied to him?

He closed the book and eyed the window. "God, if You still want to hear from a man like me, watch out for Jolene. Help her heal and move past the terror inside her." Prayer felt rusty and old, so he shifted and rolled his shoulders. If he did this, listened to the words of God and dared to believe again, he'd be all in because he knew one thing after all these years. No matter how hard he tried to overcome his failings, he couldn't. But maybe through God, he could learn and do better. If these words were true and God still loved him, then he could do better.

In the morning, he'd go with Jolene to help out at the hippotherapy program and drive her to anywhere she needed to go. To help others until maybe someday he'd figure out how to help himself. And maybe he could convince her not to devote all her energy to others and allow herself to rest to rejuvenate. To start enjoying a new hobby, cooking by his side.

He held the Bible in his lap and craved more, so he read for an hour while Jolene slept, hungry to know more, heal more, be more.

And in the dark and quiet of the night, he began to believe that he could still make a difference in the world. He'd start with helping Jolene, Logan, Bear and whoever else needed him. Jolene had been right; he'd hidden behind his mistakes long enough. Now he needed to do more. And maybe, someday, he'd be deserving of Jolene's love.

Chapter Eight

Jolene sat at the desk in the barn during Jimmy's normal therapy time looking over the rejection for the grant, but she couldn't determine what they'd done wrong. Frustrated, she sat back and rubbed her eyes free of dust. The horses were tended by Austin Wilks, and without this grant money they'd probably have to let him go next year.

She'd worked so hard that she'd collapsed on Ace last night the moment she'd arrived to spend time with him. Despite his scolding, he didn't complain. Instead, he'd tucked her in and insisted she sleep. When was the last time she'd slept that well? Not since she was able to move again.

A barn cat ran through with a meow and skittered up into the rafters. Good, the kids loved seeing the furry little one running around the place. She eyed the clock and decided she needed to head out in a few if she'd make it to the hospital to see Jimmy, to the church to help out with organizing the food drive and then to stop by to check on Ace's leg. That was if he didn't show up here first to escort her around like he'd vowed to her this morning before he took her by the hand and tucked her into her car to return to the ranch. She only hoped he'd really called the VA and set things in motion for a new prosthesis. And as long as she was stopping by to check on him, hopefully they would make dinner together.

Strange how her mind and body calmed when she hung out with him and Bear, and she found herself looking forward to the quiet end of the day instead of avoiding it with more work. Even last night, she didn't fight to stay awake. Not with him by her side. He'd been gentle and kind and giving. If only he could see the man he really was instead of the one he believed himself to be.

"Hi, you," Juniper called from behind. "You looking over the grant proposal again?"

"Yes." Jolene dropped her head into her hands and rubbed her scalp free of tension.

"Well, I have some good news. Hudson found another grant through an old company he had connections with and it could mean even more money for the program. He's been working on it nonstop. I think he felt bad about his funds being tied up with his other business and the drama with his father."

Jolene heard something in her tone that added weight to her words. "What's the catch?"

"No problem for us, but it meant Hudson had to have a conversation with his father. He's in a mood, so I thought I'd come out here." She laughed. "I love the man, and he's amazing, patient, a perfect dad to Gracie and the best husband anyone could ask for, but his father gets him worked up."

"Understood. They have a lot of history with the fight over this land and him leaving his father's shadow, but he'll calm down by dinner."

Juniper entered the office and sat in the side chair by the desk. "What about you?"

Jolene shuffled the papers, tired of people telling her she did too much. Ace had already covered that to the nth degree.

The cat scurried down and landed on the shelf and looked at them both like she wanted to join the conversation.

"What about me?" Jolene said in a summer-breeze tone.

Juniper ran her nail along a groove in the desk. "You didn't come home last night."

A flush took hold of Jolene's face. "Oh, I'm

so sorry, I should've called. I don't want to start any gossip. I fell asleep on the couch at Ace's when I went to check on Bear and I didn't wake up until this morning."

"Good."

Jolene turned her chair to face Juniper straight-on. "Good?"

"Yes, I know you don't get enough rest."

"No need to pile on. I got a lecture and a half from Ace this morning."

Juniper studied that groove awful hard. "And Ace?"

A cattle bell chimed in Jolene's head, but she couldn't avoid the question. "What about Ace?"

"You two have been spending a lot of time together. Heard you like to play ball in the park with Bear and watch birds." Her head shot up. "Don't get me wrong. I think it's good. I heard he's even been nice to people."

"I think Bear's been good for him."

Juniper tapped the desk as if to draw Jolene's attention. "And for you."

Juniper's words hung in the air for the time it took the cat to scurry off again. "We're friends."

"But there is more to it than that. I can see it in the way you smiled and laughed with the kids today. As if a part of you woke up for the first time since you'd arrived here."

Jolene straightened in her chair. "I'm sorry if you feel like I haven't done a good job."

"You know that's not what I'm saying." Juniper shifted in her chair and offered a double-brow raise. "You do know how amazing you are at your job, right?"

Jolene wanted to lighten the mood. "Of course, I know I'm awesome."

"Seriously. But there is more to life than serving everyone else."

Jolene pushed her chair back and eyed her watch. "I got sleep last night, that's all." An image of Ace on the floor, his head against the side of the couch asleep with the Bible in his hands, flashed in her mind.

"There it is. That smile that says there's more."

If she could escape the comment, she would, but Juniper wasn't just her boss, she was her friend. "Nothing really. It's just that I realized something. Ace read the Bible last night."

"And you think he's found his faith. That's great."

It was great, but not just because she'd hoped he'd found God again. Even though that was everything. A small part of her also realized that the man gave her something her family and her friends never did. He remained at her side, and if she guessed right, he'd read the Bible to her the way she'd told him she read to people at the hospital when they were unconscious. A hint of a memory of waking and him tucking her in on the couch, promising not to leave her, swelled her heart to the brim.

Jolene grabbed her purse and headed for the door. "I need to get to the hospital to visit with Jimmy. I'll be back sometime this evening. Tomorrow, we have a full day of clients. Some are new assessments, so I'll need you to help in the afternoon if you're available."

"Sure. Hudson can watch Gracie then. Oh, one more thing," Juniper called after her. "Ace called to ask permission to bring the dog by here to see how he'd behave while there were no clients, and he should be here any minute. Said he needed to see you, too."

"Me?" Jolene sounded like a squeaky barn mouse.

Juniper showed a wide, teeth-bearing smile. "That's what he said."

Jolene eyed her watch. "I can't wait. I need to go."

"Good thing I'm already here." Ace's deep, silky-yet-rumbly tone echoed in the barn office.

His words drew her to turn and face the clean-shaven man, hair freshly combed back, wearing that blue shirt she liked on him so much. But that wasn't the most distracting part; he stood in public without his prosthetic leg, leaning on a crutch.

"I know, not ideal, but when I called the VA, they warned me not to continue using the prosthesis until the wound completely healed. Also have an appointment later this week to get a new-and-improved gel sheath something or other."

"That's great." Jolene wanted to throw her arms around him and kiss him for that, but Juniper by her side and the fact that it wouldn't be appropriate at work kept her planted in her place. "I'm so sorry. I need to head off to the hospital to see Jimmy. He's really struggling."

"I told you this morning I'm going to be taking care of you today." Ace cleared his throat and nudged Bear forward; the sweet canine sat up on his hind legs with one paw in the air. "Besides, someone's been depressed and wants to get out of the house. I brought him here to see if he'd cheer up, but what do you think about us going with you into town? I called Mindi and she said Bear could hang with her, so I'm sure he can stay there while we go visit Jimmy."

Jolene didn't know what to say. Her mouth opened but no words came out so she closed it again.

"Is that okay?" he asked sheepishly. "I thought maybe he'd relate to a man with a missing limb. Sort of a wounded warrior kind of bond."

She eyed the pant leg tied up below his knee and analyzed further how the man who never allowed anyone to even see his prosthetic leg stood with his injury for all to see. Had he done this for the boy, to help him?

"Sure. I mean, yes. That would be great."

Juniper patted her shoulder. "I'll let you two get going. Don't worry about anything here. I'll take care of it. Take the rest of the day off."

"No, I'll be back later to help—"

"As your boss, I'm ordering it." Juniper nudged Jolene out the door. "Ace, take her out to dinner on us. Tell the diner to put it on our tab."

"I'll make sure she eats and is back here at a reasonable hour to get some rest."

Jolene huffed. "Who's the therapist here?"

"Woof."

"And you. Are you playing victim so Ace would take you for a ride?"

He bowed his head and scurried away but only made it so far with his leash around his neck.

With bag in hand, she joined Ace and Bear

for a ride into town. They dropped Bear off with Mindi under strict instructions he had to remain on leash and away from customers in the back room. Then Ace drove them to the hospital. But no matter how many visual prompts of happiness dotted the walls of the pediatric wing, the same sterile smell as all medical facilities haunted her.

She hated that smell.

As if Ace caught on to her tension, he placed a hand on the small of her back to keep her moving forward.

Jimmy's parents stood outside a room clinging to each other.

"Hi, how are you both holding up?" Jolene asked.

The woman with a laptop on a rolling tray nodded and then steered the cart away.

"Not so good. Jimmy is so scared of getting hurt that he refuses to leave his room to even go down the hall for therapy. They're saying they might have to discharge him if they can't get him to work with them."

Ace peered into the room, then looked back at the family before offering his hand. "I'm Ace Gatlin. Would you mind me chatting with your son for a few minutes? I might be able to help."

"I'm Luke and this is my wife, Zoey." Jimmy's father shook Ace's hand, then the couple looked to each other and then to Jolene. "If you think it'll help."

She nodded but doubt hung around her like dust in the air.

"Okay, then." Zoey lifted her chin and walked into the room with Luke on her heels. "Look who's here. It's so good of Ms. Jolene to come by to visit, right, Jimmy?"

He nodded but there was no light in his eyes. Jolene wanted to do something, anything, to make the poor kid feel better. Sometimes she didn't understand God's plan, but it wasn't her place to question it.

Look at the wonder He'd performed last night with His perfect timing. "Hi there. How's it going?" Jolene asked.

Jimmy didn't say anything, but big tears welled up in his eyes. Zoey broke down.

"Dad, why don't you take Mom for a coffee while Ace and I here visit with Jimmy."

Luke had tears in his own eyes, so he rushed out of the room and down the hall. To Jolene's surprise, Ace hobbled past her. "Hey, little man, sounds like you've had a rough time."

Jimmy looked up all the way to Ace's head towering above him. "Are you a giant?"

"No, but I pretend to be one." He leaned a little closer, holding one hand above Jimmy with his fingers arched. "Fee-fi-fo-fum, I smell a little man who needs a tickle." He poked Jimmy in the side with one finger and he squirmed, laughing.

Jolene eyed the screws in Jimmy's leg and couldn't imagine how he'd ever get back to life, but that was her job, and she'd work to make it happen.

"What happened to your leg?" Jimmy asked, pointing at the tied pant leg.

Jolene froze, not sure how Ace would handle such a question.

"I had an accident. You? What happened to your legs?"

"Same. Bad accident. I told my parents I never want to ride a bike or car or horse or tractor again."

Jolene held her breath and gritted her teeth to keep from telling him that wasn't an option because that's not what he needed to hear right now.

"Oh, I know what you mean. When I returned from my bad accident, I couldn't even leave my room."

"*You* were scared?" Jimmy's eyes went wide.

"Sure, even giants get scared."

Jimmy looked to Jolene. "You ever get scared?"

"All the time. As a matter of fact, I was scared last night."

Jimmy studied the metal contraption on his leg, then looked up at her. "What did you do?"

"I had a special giant friend who read the Bible to me." She dared a glance at Ace, who straightened and offered a big, heart-pumping grin, so she mouthed thank you to him.

Jimmy looked between them, and his little brow furrowed. "I don't get it."

Ace snapped his attention back to Jimmy. "Sometimes we just have to have faith that things will get better, but a friend can help with that."

"Are you my friend?" Jimmy asked, his forehead crinkling.

Ace pulled up a chair and sat by Jimmy's side. "I can be your giant friend who needs therapy, too."

Jimmy pointed to his missing limb. "For that?"

"Yes, and some scars you can't see. The kind that keep me from wanting to leave the house."

Jimmy shook his head and giggled. "You're not scared to leave your house."

"How do you know that?"

Jimmy rolled his eyes. "Because you're here, silly."

Ace laughed. "You are one smart boy, but what you don't know is I have a friend here, Jolene, and she helped me leave my house. It took time, and I'm still working to be better."

Jimmy looked to Jolene, who offered an affirming nod.

"Wait, I have an idea." Ace clapped his hands together once and stood up. "Jolene needs to take a phone call, but I need to go down the hall to talk to someone about a new leg and sign up for therapy. I'm awfully scared. Would you go with me?"

A speaker cut on announcing a special activity in the playroom, but Jimmy didn't move his focus from Ace and Jolene, as if letting them know he saw through them. "Alright. I mean, if you need me to stay with you the entire time, I'll go."

Jolene translated that in her head to Jimmy making sure Ace would stay with him until he returned to his room. And he did. The man sat by Jimmy while the therapist showed him how to manage his activities of daily living despite the contraption on his leg. Jolene had to keep her mouth shut, wanting to jump in to help but not wanting to cross a professional line. This was the hospital therapist's home; Jolene would have him back once he was released.

Ace escorted Jimmy back to his room, where he collapsed from exhaustion into his bed. "Will you be back tomorrow?"

Jolene held her breath. That was asking a lot of Ace, and he had other obligations to tend to, but the way Jimmy looked up to him had to touch his heart.

"I'm your giant friend. I'll be back every day here, and when you get out, I'll be at the hippotherapy program helping Ms. Jolene. Do you think you'll come visit me there?"

Jimmy smiled but his eyelids slid closed. "Yeah, I want..."

Luke and Zoey entered the room and ushered Ace and Jolene out into the hallway. Luke offered his hand to Ace. "Thank you, sir. I don't know what you did, but we sure do appreciate it."

"Not a problem. I think I got as much out of that as he did." Ace headed down the hall to the elevator; as they walked, Jolene rolled through last night and today. The fact that the man sat by her side reading to her as she'd slept, that he'd read the Bible, and now, all of this with Jimmy. She didn't know what had changed his heart, but she closed her eyes in the elevator. *Thank You, Lord. You do work wonders.*

At the bottom floor, they headed to the truck, but Jolene couldn't hold herself back a second longer. Emotions flooded to the surface and she wanted to thank Ace and show him how amazing he was, but the words didn't flow. Instead, she stood on her toes and pressed a chaste kiss to his lips.

It was quick, gentle, tender, but affirming a connection that swept her into possibilities. When she lowered and looked up at him, he had a big goofy grin plastered on his face.

"What was that for?"

"For being there for me last night, for coming along today, for what you did with Jimmy. But most of all, for you being you."

The parking lot shifted under him and he stumbled, but she caught his arm. Did Jolene see him as more than the injured, broken man that she first came to help? More than that, did he feel more put together than he had in years? "Do you kiss all your clients like that?"

"You're not my client."

He chuckled. "Well, I think Jimmy might think otherwise. I just agreed to be at the farm helping you, so I might as well be a client."

Pink tinged her cheeks, and he thought she might not realize how much he appreciated that kiss that unbalanced him. "But I hope I'm more than your client."

She nodded. "Yeah, you're more to me."

He closed the gap between them. "You're more than that to me, too."

A honk reminded him he was standing in a hospital parking lot, so he reached behind her and opened the door. "We should pick up Bear so we can get home to work on dinner."

"Right. Let's go." Jolene sat in the passenger seat with fingers laced together in her lap until they left the parking lot and she slid her hand to the center where Bear usually sat.

His heart beat against his ribs, but he wouldn't let his fear win, so he reached across and took her offering, raised her arm and kissed her palm. "Maybe after we settle Bear, you would honor me with a date?"

"Just the two of us?" she asked in a breathy tone.

"That's usually how a date works," he teased.

At the end of the street, he turned down Main and headed to the florist shop.

"I'd like that," she said, then bit her lip.

"But?"

"No *buts*." She squeezed his hand. "I'm just so proud of you and want to enjoy the moment and not push you too fast."

He pulled into a parking lot and turned off the engine to face her. "Don't do that."

"What?"

"I thought we agreed you're not my therapist. It's not up to you if I'm okay, it's up to me. And I'm doing well and plan to keep working at it. I even called Logan this morning and he'll be coming here for a few weeks while we catch up and I help him figure some things out."

"You did?" Jolene asked.

"I did. Now, will you be my date Saturday night?"

She smiled, the first genuine smile he'd seen, and it was breathtakingly beautiful. "Yes."

"Good."

"Woof. Woof."

Bear raced to the truck with the leash trailing behind him. Mindi ran out, her hair disheveled and her apron twisted. "Sorry, I opened the door and I couldn't stop him."

Jolene bent down and took the leash. "Bear, are you not behaving? I thought you were all mopey and depressed."

"No, he's been good, following me around the back room with his tail wagging."

"Good, guess he's out of his funk. Thanks again for watching him for us."

"No problem. Anytime." Mindi hugged Jolene, waved to Ace, then retreated back to the shop.

Ace rounded the truck and climbed in, sliding his crutch behind the seat and pulling himself up one last time. Bear licked his face. "I'm glad to see you, too, but cut it out. I have to drive."

Bear looked at each of them, then jumped over Jolene to her other side, forcing her to slide to the middle.

"Did you train him to be your wingman?" Jolene asked.

"No, he learned that all on his own. I think he's playing matchmaker."

"Woof."

Jolene covered her ear. "No, too loud. Inside bark, please."

Bear settled in Jolene's normal seat, so Ace reached around her and took the lap belt, then hooked it in place. She watched him, her lips only inches from his own, but he didn't kiss her. Not now. He wanted to treat her the way she deserved, romantic and cherished and like the gift she was to the world.

He drove them home, where he taught her how to make a simple chicken noodle soup. To his relief, he discovered there was a lot about cooking he needed to teach her.

For the next three days, he woke without a nightmare, went to Kenmore farm to help with hippotherapy, drove to the hospital to read to patients and visit with Jimmy and went to church to help with packaging food. On day four, he drove four hours to Nashville for his new leg so that on Saturday he could walk better on his date with Jolene.

Friday came and he strutted into the barn, where Jimmy waited for his first time around the corral. The boy had become his fast friend, teaching Ace about life more than he ever thought possible. He had never been so happy to get out of bed in the morning, and the world seemed brighter. He'd even spoken to Logan a few more times, and the idea of having his friend live with him while he focused on getting back on his feet became more appealing to Ace. Maybe God really was working in his heart and his life.

"Okay, Jimmy. You ready for a pony ride? Ms. Jolene says maybe next week you can move up to the horse."

Jolene came out of her office and nodded, but Jimmy's gaze didn't leave Ace.

"I'm not ready for that." Jimmy blinked up at Ace, his little face so sweet and innocent and hopeful. "Am I?"

"No one will push you. Let's just go for a

stroll around the corral and show your mom and dad how brave you are."

Juniper brought a riding client inside the barn and waited for them to move away from the mounting and dismounting steps.

"Mom and Dad haven't smiled in a while. Maybe this will help them be happy again." Jimmy looked at the pony. "It's my fault. They used to be so happy before my accident. If I didn't disobey the rules and leave my yard, then I wouldn't have two bad legs and my parents wouldn't be sad."

Ace's chest tightened. "Oh, bud. Accidents happen." He adjusted Jimmy's helmet. "It's what we do to overcome those accidents that makes us the people we are. And know this—you might have disobeyed the rules, but your mom and dad love you, and all kids make mistakes. It's part of growing up. You're a good kid, Jimmy, and you deserve to heal and run and play again."

"You think so?" The little man's chin trembled, tugging at those invisible heartstrings that had recently grown in Ace.

"I know so. Now come on, let's go show you off."

Jimmy adjusted in the seat, and after making sure he was snug and strapped in, Ace walked the pony out to the corral to Jimmy's clapping parents. Jolene joined them, spotting Jimmy from the other side; as the official therapist, she had to be involved anyway.

"Good job, Jimmy," Mom called out.

Dad raised his fist in the air. "That's my boy."

Jimmy lifted his chin and glowed with triumph so bright it warmed Ace to the core. After several laps, they guided Jimmy back to the stable to dismount and congratulated him on a job well done.

Jimmy's parents came inside and Jolene walked over to speak to them. "Stay in the saddle a minute. Ace?"

"I've got him. No worries." Ace turned to tie the rope to the post to make sure the pony didn't move.

Thud. "Ow!"

Ace spun and found Jimmy on the ground, fallen from the pony. His leg was bleeding where the screws had been.

Jolene, Juniper and Jimmy's mom and dad all rushed over. Ace stumbled out of the way. He gasped for oxygen, caught between terror and failure. *No. No. No.*

God. Please help Jimmy. What had he been thinking trying to assist people, especially a child? He'd been selfish, trying to prove himself worthy of a woman like Jolene. He wasn't worthy.

The barn closed in around him, his breath like fire in his lungs. His gut twisted.

A door creaked, a blast, gunfire, the smell of blood and charred wood. The barn spun and he thought he'd be sick. He hunched over the hay, gasping, unable to look back at Jimmy but trying to stay on the farm and not slip back into war and death.

He heaved and panted, but the sounds and the smells and the taste of war coated every sense.

Sirens sounded in the distance, but he retreated from what he'd done, from Jolene calling out to him, from the world. A world in which he only caused chaos and pain. So he ran. Ran from everything he'd allowed himself to dream he could have only to now face the truth. He belonged where he couldn't harm anyone with his bad decisions. He belonged alone.

Chapter Nine

Jolene pulled up to Ace's house. He'd disappeared so fast, but she'd seen it. The look on his face. He'd retreated, so she needed to coax him out again. To show him accidents happen, that he didn't have to carry the burden of a mistake.

Knock. Knock. Knock.

"Woof."

"Hey, Bear, tell Ace I'm coming in," she shouted to make sure that she didn't enter without warning, but the door wouldn't budge. "Ace, unlock the door. We need to talk."

No response.

"Listen, Jimmy's fine. It wasn't your fault. He unhooked the strap and tried to get down for himself. If it was anyone's fault, it's mine. I'm the therapist. I'm responsible for all the clients." She pressed her palm to the door, willing him to open before he shut himself away for good.

No answer. Okay, change in tactics. Anything to get him to talk to her.

"He's upset because he knows he did the wrong thing again. Maybe you could speak with him. He listens to you."

"It wasn't his fault. I'm the one who let him fall," he said, his voice distant, as if lost somewhere far away.

"No, you weren't at fault. Stop taking the blame." She banged on the door, needing him to see the truth. "Don't do this. Jimmy's going to be fine. No damage to his legs, only three stitches to his wound to reclose it. He's asking for you."

"He's better off without me," he said so softly she could barely make out his words. They sounded as broken as she knew he felt.

"Please, open the door." Jolene rested her forehead against the cool wood, willing him to come out and not lock himself away again. "We need to take Bear for a walk in town today. There's only seven days left until the festival and the deadline to prove to the state that a dog with PTSD can be rehabilitated and doesn't need to be euthanized."

No response. "I thought you could teach me how to make a turkey today. And maybe tackle bread. I'm really enjoying learning to cook."

No response. She pounded her fists against the door. "Don't do this. Don't leave me alone again." Her words shattered and scattered along with her heart.

He mumbled something, but she couldn't make out his words as if he faded farther and farther away from her.

"Fine, I'll give you some space. I'll see you tomorrow night for our date." Jolene backed away, hoping by then he'd recover. "If you want to talk, text me. I'm here for you. Not as your therapist or friend but because I care about you, Ace Gatlin." There, she'd said it aloud; he'd show tomorrow because there was no way he'd sacrifice how far they'd come together.

She went home and prayed like she'd never prayed before. In the morning, she didn't go over to Ace's house because she needed to wait and see what he'd do. To let him figure things out for himself because only he could do the work to get better.

When afternoon came, there were still no texts, but she had faith in him so she put on her best dress, then waited outside the barn for him.

And waited.

And waited.

And waited.

When the sun dipped below the horizon, she knew the truth. What Ace had said that day weeks ago was true. She couldn't save everyone. Nothing she did would change him because only he could change himself.

She shuffled up the stairs to her apartment and fell onto the bed, tears streaming down her cheeks. "God, why? I'm trying so hard, and I believed You were working on his heart, opening it. I thought I'd found the man You designed for me, to love me and fill that space that has been there for so long." She held her Bible to her chest, aching for warmth and love. And she realized the only way to fill that hole inside her was to turn it over to God, so she did. She got in her car and drove to Ace's house and placed her Bible in front of the door. And she walked away.

And this time, she wouldn't try to help because she'd given it her all. And she had nothing left to give. Weighted with fear to face her life alone once more, she drove home and sat on her bed, too scared to go to sleep because the feeling of waking trapped, able to hear but unable to talk with anyone, plagued her. After an hour, she forced herself to lie down and closed her eyes. For whatever tomorrow brought, only God knew.

Ace pressed his palm to the door, wishing he could touch Jolene, but he'd lost that right.

At her retreating footsteps, he peered through the front window curtains to watch her go to her car. She was dressed in a beautiful flowing dress, hair pulled up, and he knew she'd gone all out as he had for their date. Up before dawn, he'd done all his chores, cleaned up, changed and put on that shirt he knew she liked so much, trying to convince himself he was up to it, that he could be in her life. But when he'd picked up his keys and headed for his truck, he couldn't do it. He wasn't able to face her.

Now, watching her dressed and ready for their date, he was convinced that if he looked up *worst man in the world* on the internet, he'd find his picture.

Jolene drove away, but he still waited a few minutes before opening the door. He stepped out and kicked a book. Not just any book.

Her Bible.

His body drained of heat. She'd left him her most important treasure. He picked it up, knowing this was all she had in her life when she faced the darkness of the night, yet she'd left it for him. A tremor erupted in his gut. If only he could be the man she deserved.

Bear whined in the corner and gave him a you're-a-fool glower before settling back down facing the corner. He hadn't even licked Ace's face or brought him a ball all day. Maybe he felt the loss of Jolene as much as Ace did. Doubtful, because a bomb-sized hole was all that remained of Ace's heart.

She was better off without him because she deserved a man worthy of her love and goodness. Not that such a man existed. And the thought of another man in her life twisted his resolve, but he wanted to do the right thing for once and let her go.

Tomorrow, he'd return her Bible and Bear, so they'd both be better off. With one glance at his furry friend, he knew he'd failed him, too.

Bible in hand, he went upstairs, tossed it on the mattress, changed out of his dress clothes and collapsed onto the bed, the Bible resting against his side.

No. He'd already fallen for that; it wouldn't happen again. He set it on the nightstand and forced himself to sleep so he didn't have to face the world for a few hours.

But only an hour later he jolted awake. "Jimmy," he cried out.

Heaving, he looked at the clock. 1:22 a.m. Great, he couldn't escape his life even in sleep. No way he'd wait for his typical 4:22 a.m. wake-up terror when he already had to relive Jimmy's fall.

He sat on the side of the bed with head in hands until his pulse slowed and his lungs didn't feel like they were on fire.

Jolene's Bible sat mocking him from the nightstand at his side, so he grabbed it and headed downstairs.

With cup of coffee in hand, he sat at the kitchen table and eyed the old, worn book. "Not falling for that again. You made me believe I was worthy of love, but I'm not."

Silence. If only he had Jolene's faith. The kind that got a person through medically induced social isolation. The thought of being trapped inside a body that didn't move or breathe on its own shook him. She'd said she'd only survived through her faith. He didn't know how she survived that at all. That's more than any person should ever have to face yet she came out the other side and still had more to give the world.

He patted the book. "How do I have that, God?"

No answer. Not that he expected a booming voice to echo through the room but he craved something, a sign.

A rumble of thunder answered him. "Right, I'm in a life storm. Got it. But I've been in rough weather for so long. Will there ever be an end?"

Nothing.

Again.

Maybe Jolene was right and it's listening to or reading God's word that possesses healing power, so he slid the Bible to rest directly in front of him. "Okay, God. Tell me, what do I need to do? How do I do better?"

He opened the book where one of the ribbons held a spot and found an outlined passage. He saw the same passage, 1 John 4:16.

He thought of being a child and having his grandparents tell him over and over again why he needed to study math, though he didn't understand why. "Seriously? This is all you've got? Love? You're love?"

Bear whined and whimpered in the other room.

Ace shoved the Bible from him and went to check on Bear. "What's wrong, buddy?"

He didn't even lift his head.

"I know. I'll figure out where to take you tomorrow, where you'll do better. I'm sorry I can't help you."

He sat on the floor by Bear and leaned his head back against the wall. At some point, he fell asleep until the next night terror took hold.

Work. He needed to work, so at the first ray of light, he changed and headed out to exhaust himself until he could feel nothing again, but

Bear didn't come when he called. He remained sulking in a corner.

Ace spent hours in the barn and then returned to the house for lunch, but when he opened the door, Bear bolted.

"Bear!" Ace darted after him.

A furry blur jumped into the woods toward the east side of the property where three farms—Kenmore, Snyder and his farmland—joined at the corner.

Just when he thought life couldn't get any worse. He walked as fast as he could, but still getting used to the new leg hampered his progress. Drenched in sweat, he reached Benjamin Snyder's fence and listened but didn't hear him screaming or yelling or Bear barking.

"Bear, where are you?" He hiked up and down the fence until he reached the end on the north side.

"Woof."

It was distant and soft, but he knew that bark anywhere. "I'm coming. Stay there."

He hobbled through the dense brush and stumbled over a root, knocking his head into a stump. Blood oozed from his temple, but he managed to pull himself up again and keep going. Again and again, he stumbled but kept getting back up each time he heard Bear bark.

Until he reached the north corner of the fence and saw Bear running in the open field around a cow with Jolene laughing and clapping. He stood there, blood dripping from his face, his shirt and pants torn.

Hudson and Juniper joined her, along with Gracie. The dog ran up and rolled over on his back to let Gracie pet his belly. He looked happy and home.

A storybook family unveiled in the distance and he wanted to step out of the shadows, to be a part of so much joy. He wanted to feel the touch of Jolene's lips, hear the sound of their child laughing, feel the warmth of her against him in the night as they held each other through their worst fears.

And she could have that. All of it. A life full of happiness and comfort; he would never deny her that. He saw it now, what God was telling him. There wasn't a doubt in his mind that he loved that woman—the one who drew out his darkness and shined light on his soul—but that didn't mean he could have her. There was enough of God's love to go around, but that's all he'd have. God showed him what being a good person meant, and how he could help others, but only within his limitations. An old friend he could bring home to help until he recovered, sure. But a child? No, a child would be too delicate. Jolene was too special to be in his world.

So he turned around and walked home, holding his love close to his heart, but he wouldn't let it out. He'd let them go so that they could be happy. That's all he wanted. "Dear Lord, please give me strength and give Jolene the peace and love she deserves."

Chapter Ten

A feeling of someone watching her drew Jolene's attention to the tree line toward Ace's property. She thought she saw movement through the trees but it could've been an animal.

"Do you think Ace knows Bear's here?" Hudson asked.

Jolene slid her phone from her pocket. "No messages." She typed out a quick one and waited.

A thumbs-up. That's all she got.

Her chest ached and her limbs were heavy with sorrow, but she had no choice but to keep a smile on her face and keep moving forward. "He knows, but he's not coming to get him."

Bear zipped in and out and ran around flipping and showing off for a giggling Gracie. "We still need to be careful. He's really lovable and friendly, but he did attack Benjamin Snyder when he charged Ace with a shotgun. My theory is the gun is Bear's trigger, or maybe a sound or anything that reminds him of the night his handler was killed, but we haven't tested the idea yet. I'd planned to do that today, but it's best not to try it here. Since he's doing better, I trust him not to be a problem if I keep him in my apartment until morning and then do my best to convince Ace to take him back. If that's okay with you."

"Of course. Look at him and Gracie. He's so sweet and gentle with her," Juniper said.

Jolene already knew it would be an impossible job to convince Ace, but she had to try. They shouldn't have Bear here long term; the liability with the kids would be too high. "I hate to say it, but we have a full calendar today so he'll have to remain in my apartment alone all day."

Hudson eyed his giggling daughter. "Tell you what. I'll try to take him back to Ace now. If not, I'll keep him away until the last client leaves. I'm sure we can hang together at the park and run some errands."

"That would be great. Thanks." Jolene hoped someone else might be able to get through to Ace where she'd failed. "Just keep him on leash at all times, please."

"That is if you can get him away from Gracie," Juniper laughed.

"As Jolene said, until we are a hundred percent, Gracie shouldn't be around him." Hudson whistled loud enough to hurt Jolene's ear for a second but it did the trick. Bear ran like a rabbit to Hudson with his hop run. He'd really learned to get around on three legs. If only humans could adapt that quickly.

They all headed back to the house. Hudson retrieved his keys and Jolene sat on the porch petting Bear. "He abandoned you, too, huh? It's okay. He promised he'd never abandon me and he did. We'll figure something out."

The door opened behind her, so she stood up to let Hudson pass. "Want to go for a ride?"

Bear jumped and flipped and raced to the nearest vehicle. When Hudson unlocked his doors with a ding, Bear trotted over and jumped in with only a little extra effort. Jolene stayed in her spot watching them drive away, praying not only Hudson but also God would get through to Ace.

"Don't worry, Hudson's good at convincing people to do things. He convinced me to marry him." Juniper clearly read the worries on Jolene's face.

Jolene laughed but despite her momentary happiness watching Bear and Gracie, she didn't feel much like enjoying anything. "Best get to work." She checked her schedule and helped Austin with the new saddle designed for hip issues for her postsurgical patient who wanted to get back to riding.

She managed to get through her first appointment with only a few glances at the long drive to see if Hudson returned with Ace and Bear. Next up was a mother of four who wanted to take her kids on a trip out west but was petrified of horses. Third, a young boy who had cerebral palsy. It's what she loved about her job, helping so many different needs with one modality.

The work helped soothe Jolene's aching heart, and when she reached her appointment with Gracie, a little extra light shone in her day. Her star client who'd made so much progress always made her remember why she worked so hard for so many people.

Today, they focused on hand grip by holding the reins, which she did perfectly, despite crying every time someone put a pencil or pen in her hand. Gracie had already increased gross motor control by working her core on horseback. Even her speech had improved, and she'd learned the alphabet and spelling while on horseback. Jolene and Juniper had even managed to get her to read signs they'd placed around the barn while she moved, cleaning and stacking things. As long as she was being stimulated, she learned things quickly.

Jolene kept reminding herself all day how much she loved her job, but then why wasn't it enough? She should be happy with what she had. Part of her wanted more, though. All of it. The fairy-tale happily-ever-after with Ace.

But he was no prince and she never fooled herself into thinking he was. He was special, though, and she loved special people.

After Gracie finished, Hudson returned, and when she heard Bear bark, she knew he'd wasted his time going over to Ace's place.

Jolene walked out to bring Bear up to her apartment until she could see her last three clients while avoiding a liability issue. "Didn't get him to agree?"

"Didn't find him. His truck's there but the men said he went out to work and hadn't returned."

"Punishing himself. Probably working until he irritates his wound again." She shook her head and sighed. "Come on, boy, let's get you settled. I'll try tomorrow." Despite the fact that it was the last thing she wanted to do.

She opened the apartment door and put a blanket on the floor, but Bear stood watching her with that sweet tilt of his head. "Sorry, you've got to stay here, buddy."

He sank with a whine, so she sat down on

the floor with him for a few moments. She had a little time to spare since her client called to say he'd be late. "I know he's a good man." She eyed the wilted and dried-out flowers in the pumpkin he'd personally designed for her, which she hadn't had the heart to throw out. "I mean, those flowers were the sweetest thing ever, don't you think?"

Bear didn't respond or move.

"And cooking dinners. And the reading to me. I know he cares about me, but I can't fix him. He can only fix himself. And something tells me I need to give up on that because he'll never believe himself worthy of love."

For the rest of the day, she did everything she could to focus on work and not her personal life, until night came. But as if Bear sensed her struggle to sleep, he hopped up on the bed and snuggled into her side. "Thanks. I can't promise that I can get him to take you back, but I can try."

A whine and a cuddle later, Bear snored at her side, and although she relaxed and dozed in and out, she never slept as well as she did that night that Ace sat by her side reading the Bible to her.

When dawn came, she got ready for her day and drove Bear to Ace's house. She knocked but he didn't come to the door. "I'm not leaving until you answer, so you better open this door."

"Woof."

"You tell him," Jolene said, holding on to his leash.

The door flew open to a disheveled, dark circle-eyed Ace. He looked rough. Probably from working so much and not sleeping. Hypocrite much?

"I had to get my leg on."

She wanted to ask if it was because he opened his wounds, but she wouldn't. If he wanted help, he'd have to ask for it this time. "You need to keep your agreement and take Bear back here for at least one more week."

Ace eyed Bear. "No."

Bear whined and plopped down.

"You made a promise, and you know I can't keep him at the Kenmore ranch. It's too much liability with the hippotherapy program, not to mention Gracie."

"You don't get it. He doesn't belong here. The poor dog has been miserable. He ran off to be with you guys."

She wanted to shake him and tell him he was being unreasonable but he'd only balk further. "Listen. He needs you. If you don't take him, they'll put him down."

"Don't be dramatic. You'll find him a home. That's what you do, you help everyone."

"Everyone that will accept my help." She huffed, frustration welling up inside her.

He stepped out onto the porch, towering over her as if he could intimidate her, but she knew better; the man wouldn't hurt anyone. "Let me be clear. I'm not interested, and I never will be. It was fun to entertain the idea for a while, but I'm a confirmed old bachelor who doesn't enjoy people invading his space. Now you both should leave."

Her lip trembled, so she sucked it between her teeth and bent down to buy a moment to collect herself under the guise of petting Bear. "Did you hear that? We're on our own again."

Ace retreated into the house and shut the final door with a thud. She wanted to scream at him that he was a coward, but all she managed was to say, "Thanks for making me believe there was one person in this world that would be there and never leave me alone, only to abandon me."

She left. Left the world of Ace Gatlin and his empty promises.

Quiet. Mind-numbing, unnerving quiet. Not even the sound of a coyote howled outside. Ace had once coveted his peace and embraced being alone in the world but that was before he'd met Jolene and Bear.

The corner where Bear had slept was empty since he'd given the bed he bought to Hudson when he'd come by to convince him to take Bear in again, and Ace might have checked outside a few dozen times to see if he'd run back home. But he'd made his choice.

Smart dog.

Unable to face his bedroom, he dozed on the couch with the television on, hearing tales about storms out west and a shooting up north. "God, why is the world this way? Why do we hurt one another?"

Wind whipped outside and a drizzle clinked against the front porch roof. The sound that soothed him, like the night he'd sat by Jolene reading to her while she slept on this couch.

He rubbed his chest; the ache had settled so deep he thought it went through his spine. Despite the leg fitting better, he'd planned on working with Jolene to learn to use it, so he'd opted out of his physical therapy at the VA again. Technology had changed, and it was lighter and easier to walk, but that meant he swung his leg too far and had an uneven stride.

His phone dinged so he rolled over and picked it up off the coffee table. Not Jolene.

A tight squeeze constricted his heart, but he forced himself to read the text from Logan.

I'll be there in a few weeks. Thank you. I had almost given up on life before you reached out.

Was it true? Had he helped someone? Maybe it was easy for him to help a fellow veteran. But not a little boy. That was different.

He closed his eyes and saw Jimmy on the ground, so he stood and went to the kitchen table, grabbed his keys and reached for the leash that was gone...before he realized he didn't have Bear to take with him anymore.

Good, they wouldn't allow him in the hospital anyway. Life returned to simpler times; it would only take him a few days to get used to it.

Rain pelted down by the time he reached the hospital administration office. He flipped his raincoat hood off and went inside. "Excuse me, where's billing?"

"Down the hall, third door on the right." The lady pointed with a pen and he followed her directions.

No one waited in line, probably due to the rain, so he waltzed up to the counter with his credit card and checkbook in hand.

A woman lowered her glasses down her nose and looked up at him. "How can I help you, sir?"

"I'd like to pay a bill."

"What's the account number?"

Ace shifted his hip to relieve the muscle cramp in his backside. "Don't have it."

"Okay, date of birth?"

He held his hand next to his hip. "This tall, what would that be? I don't know kids."

Her brows furrowed and she removed her glasses, setting them on the desk. "Sir, I need some information if I'm going to help. Can you at least give me a name?"

"Yeah, it's Jimmy."

Her keys went clickety-clack and stopped. "Last name?"

"He was here a few weeks ago for surgery, then back two days ago for a fall from a pony. I just want to pay anything that the insurance didn't cover."

"Are you a relative?" she asked.

"No."

"Then I can't help you, sir."

Ace pressed his palms to the counter. "But I'm paying a bill, not asking for personal information."

"Yes, but I can't access the account."

"I can promise the parents won't mind if you look him up so I can pay his bill. No one would ever mind someone paying their bill for them."

"Maybe so, but I can't locate the child without further information."

Ace grunted but knew whom he could call. "I'll be back."

"Sir, you don't have to come here." She slapped a card up on the counter. "Call this number, give them the account number or last name and pay it on the phone."

He snagged it, shoved it in his pocket and headed home. On the way, he knew he could call Jolene to ask for the information, but that wasn't a good idea. He needed time and distance until he could see her without falling at her feet and begging her to give him another chance.

He'd vowed not to do that, to let her go to find someone better, so he dialed Hudson. He'd be able to look up the information for him.

The phone rang, echoing in his empty truck, accentuating the loss of his canine and female companions.

"Hello, Ace. What can I do for you?" Hudson sounded bland, direct, not his usual friendly persona.

"Yes, I need some help with something."

Hudson cleared his throat. "Okay, what do you need help with?"

"I need Jimmy's last name." Ace turned onto Main Street to head home. Once he paid the bill, he'd work on cleaning out the spare room for Logan.

A poignant pause.

"Hudson?"

"Yeah, uh, what for?"

That wasn't his normal delivery. Maybe he didn't want to get involved.

"Listen, don't tell anyone, please. And I mean no one. But I just want to pay Jimmy's outstanding bill that his insurance doesn't cover. I have the means, and it was my fault."

"Ace, it wasn't—"

"Are you going to tell me or not? Oh, and I need his date of birth, too." Ace maneuvered around a puddle forming in a pothole and drifted back into his lane, waiting for Hudson.

"Give me a minute."

Ace waited for over a minute for him to return, but he eventually shared the information.

"Thanks, man." Ace should hit End, but the fool he was, he couldn't help himself. "How are they doing?"

"Jimmy?"

"Yes, and…the others."

"What others?" Hudson asked.

"Right. I get it. None of my business. Just do me one more favor. Let me know if either of them need anything. Anything at all."

"Anonymously, you mean?" Hudson said in a flat tone.

"Yeah, I'd appreciate it."

The rain slowed, but the creek rose enough to force him into four-wheel drive to get down the drive.

"We can't keep Bear. You know that, right?" Hudson's voice deepened to agitation.

"Yes, it's next on my list to try to find him a home. I know how busy you all are. Sorry I wasn't the man for the job," he added as if it explained his behavior.

Voices sounded in the background, so Ace cleared his throat. "Gotta go." He hung up before he reached the house and went inside. With the storm, he stayed trapped inside the rest of the day, which was torture.

During the morning, he made calls, paid bills and cleared out the room. The billing lady didn't even suspect he wasn't a family member, so it only took minutes to pay Jimmy's bill. It wasn't nominal, but he was glad he had the means to pay it.

A selfish part of him felt good for helping, even if from a distance. Maybe he could aid some more families in the area with donations. Maybe he could give some money to hippotherapy. He had more than he needed. The farm had done well, and his inheritance from his grandparents just sat in an account, not to mention his military benefits and income from the feed store.

Maybe when Logan arrived, they could look into doing something with veterans. They could start some sort of work program here at the farm.

A dog barked outside, sending Ace's heart soaring. Had he chosen to come home? Ace raced down the stairs, not wanting to leave Bear outside in the rain, but when he opened the door, there was no animal there.

Great, he was hearing things now.

Besides, it wasn't like Bear could run off since he'd be leashed or in a crate.

The afternoon droned on for as long as a Willow Oaks rezoning meeting. He paced and walked and watched television, tried to read, but nothing could get rid of the gnawing feeling that something was wrong.

When evening came, he settled onto the couch to eat his dinner. After he ate, he made his way out to the front porch for some fresh air, but when he sat on the swing, his mind went to holding Jolene and watching the stars. The stars were grayed out by the storm clouds like his life grayed in her absence.

The rain picked back up, so he enjoyed a good storm, but when the precipitation came sideways, chilling him, he returned to the shelter of his empty home. He flicked on the television but apparently something had happened because all he got was white snow.

Bored. Alone. Trapped by the rain. Nowhere to go, no one to see. No television to watch.

He retrieved his whittling tools but when he found the unfinished one Jolene had worked on, he lost interest in creating anything so he went to the kitchen. Perhaps making some cookies would soothe his mood, but before he even reached the stove his mind wandered to Jolene in his grandmother's apron chopping vegetables.

Great, all the things he loved to do were now tainted by memories of Jolene. Renovations, which is how he'd spent most of his time prior to Jolene and Bear, hadn't been scarred with memories, but passion for taking on a new project didn't entice him at all. None of his former life appealed to him at the moment. What was left?

He spotted the Bible on the table, mocking him. *Really? Are You trying to tell me something? I get it, You love me, but that doesn't mean I'm worthy of Jolene or Bear. You better than anyone should know that, Lord. I'm not a churchgoing, on-my-knees, humble kind of man. I'm undeserving and unable to change. Look at what I did to poor little Jimmy.*

No answer. Only the book. The Bible.

"Fine." He sat down and picked up the old, worn black book and turned it backward and forward, flipping pages, working the spine a little so he could come up with a new passage, then set it down. His leg tapped the edge of the table and sent the book to the floor with a thump.

He looked down and saw that the book had fallen open to 1 John 4:16.

Chapter Eleven

Dinner had no taste despite Hudson's excellent cooking. Jolene pushed her casserole around with a fork, unable to stomach another bite.

Gracie bounced on her knees. "I play Bear."

Juniper looked to Hudson, who shook his head. "No, hon, we explained that he's still recovering and needs to rest. Once we figure some things out, we'll see what we can do, but for now you need to promise not to be around him."

Gracie collapsed onto her heels and stuck out her lip. "He good dog."

"Any progress on finding Bear a permanent home?" Juniper asked with a pleading glance.

Jolene wanted to fall back and stick out her own lip. "No. I'm afraid not. Ace had been the best option until Bear is fully cleared." His name churned her stomach, so she nudged her plate away, not able to tolerate the smell of the cheese and peppery aroma.

"I excuse, please?" Gracie asked.

"Sure, but go pick up your room before you can have iPad time," Hudson said in a firm but soft tone.

Gracie sulked out of the room, arms hung low, shoulders down. She was a sweet girl with so much personality. Jolene thought of the three of them as family, but was she really just a guest? Would they stick around if she ever needed someone? They were good people but not family. Not really.

But family didn't mean anything.

Great, Ace had her questioning everything.

"Do you think he'll change his mind?" Hudson stood and cleared his and Gracie's plates.

"No. I'm going to have to find Bear a home once he's officially cleared."

"That's not what he's asking." Juniper scooted into Gracie's chair by Jolene's side. "We know how you two feel about each other. I'll be the first to admit that I had my concerns about you being with him because all I'd seen was his gruff side, but you showed me that he's more than just a bitter man. There's no denying it. You're both good for each other."

Jolene raised a brow. "We've never even been on a real date, so it's not a big deal." But it was a big deal. They'd shared more between them than she had with any man on any date in her life.

Juniper toyed with her napkin in her lap. "Maybe he's shy and needs a nudge."

Jolene sighed. "No. He won't ask because he needs to keep everyone at a distance. He doesn't trust himself and feels like he'll fail someone, so he hides from everyone. If it hadn't been Jimmy's fall, it would've been something else. Eventually, Ace Gatlin will always close himself off from the world." *And from me.* No way she'd ever be with a man who would leave her. But did everyone leave at some point?

She stood and headed for her apartment. "Thanks for dinner. I'm going to retire early. Didn't get much sleep last night trying to figure out what to do with Bear."

"Do you really think they'll put him down if he doesn't do well on his final test and you can't find him a permanent safe home?" Hudson asked. The man was kind and caring but Jolene knew he was torn between being supportive and protecting his daughter.

"Don't know." She paused. "Listen. I think my only other option is to move off the farm."

Hudson looked to Juniper, who stood by his side.

Jolene looked at them both and thought a young newlywed couple with a daughter who had a developmental disability could use some more privacy anyway. "I know that the apartment is part of my extras, but I think it might be my only option to save Bear. And that's only if I can finish training him and determine his trigger for sure."

"We'd be sorry for you to move away." Juniper cleared the rest of the dishes, as if busying herself to avoid the conversation.

Hudson took the plates and put them in soapy water. "We can add a living stipend to your salary."

"I know the budget, and that isn't in there," Jolene protested.

He smiled. "We have other funds, and maybe you can watch Gracie on occasion and we'll call it even."

"I could do that, but I hate for you to pay out of your own pocket." Translation: Jolene couldn't be the cause of him making another call to his father. A man who'd tried to take his money to save his own company, claiming that Hudson held responsibilities as partial owner in his enterprise. All manipulation, but that was how his father worked. Something she understood given her own childhood.

Juniper laughed. "He's got deep pockets. We might choose to live our lives modestly but don't worry about a little extra monthly expense. His father's deal came through and he's released Hudson's funds. The legal drama is over. But we really do wish you'd stay. You're part of our family now."

Could that be true? No, it's a friendly thing to say and they were friends. The best of friends. But not family.

"Maybe you can rent the apartment to someone to offset the cost." Jolene shuffled out the front door to a whirlwind of leaves swirling in the yard from the wind. Dark clouds loomed in the distance, so she retreated to her apartment, where Bear curled up next to her as if he knew she couldn't sleep without him there.

As much as it was convenient living here, and included in her salary as free board, there had to be something she could find that wouldn't be too expensive. Her parents had plenty, but their money would come with conditions. They'd thought her therapy work would be a phase and she'd return to their lifestyle, but she had no desire to be a socialite who traveled the world. She didn't like taking Hudson's personal money, either, but if it saved Bear, she might not have a choice.

She grabbed her cell phone and did a search for rentals in the area, but in the small town of Willow Oaks, it was more about word of mouth than advertising on the internet, so she texted Mindi. If you hear of any rooms for rent or apartments, can you let me know?

Jolene rested her head back, listening to the wind howling outside. It would be another long and lonely night of darkness where she'd sleep with the light on.

Her phone buzzed, so she checked the message.

Who's looking? Mindi asked.

Me.

Why are you leaving Kenmore ranch?

That was a loaded question she didn't want to answer, but she did need to give a reason so Mindi would try her best to help. Need a place to live with Bear.

I'm sorry.

Jolene didn't mind, though. She liked Bear's company, and it wouldn't be a bad thing to be closer to town when she wanted to help at the hospital or church. It's fine. I'll still work here.

A distant train sound echoed over tracks. She always enjoyed listening to the train in the distance rumble and toot its horn.

A clap of thunder warned her not to go outside to hear it better or she'd get soaked by rain coming their way. Soon, outside would match the raging storm inside her heart. Why couldn't the man move on with his life, a life with her in it? Bitterness sizzled inside, but she closed her eyes and said a quick prayer because that attitude wouldn't get her anywhere.

Her phone dinged with two simple words that brought so much heartache. About Ace...

Jolene tensed. Does everyone know? Great, with the entire town knowing it would be hard to move on easily. But she would. This was his choice, so she couldn't change it.

Mindi responded, It's a small town.

Jolene rubbed her aching head. Perfect.

In case you wanted to know, town is pro-Ace. They want you two to work things out.

Tell the town there is no Ace and me. Let me know if you find something. Bye. She didn't mean to be rude, but this was one conversation she didn't want to have with anyone, not even her friend.

Bear whined and lifted his head.

"Don't worry, boy, I'll make this work. It'll be you and me. At least we'll have each other. You won't abandon me, will you?"

"Woof."

The sky opened and dumped a torrential downpour.

Thud. Thud. Thud.

The sound hammered over her head so loud she thought she should crawl under her bed for protection.

"Woof. Woof."

"It's hail, buddy. Nothing to worry about. You're inside, safe. My car, on the other hand..." she joked, but apparently Bear didn't find it funny because he bolted up and barked and jumped and growled at the window.

"Calm down. It's okay." She reached for him to ease his anxiety.

Bear snarled and snapped.

Her pulse quickened, and she yanked her hand back. "Take a breath. No one's going to hurt us."

The roar of the train intensified. "It's just a train."

She spun and faced the window. The roaring of the engine grew loud as if the train had jumped the tracks and headed straight for them. Every muscle in her body tensed.

"Woof! Woof! Woof!"

The room shook. She stumbled back, falling onto the bed. Something slammed into the wall outside. A crack fissured down the plaster.

Bear bit her pant leg and tugged, growling as if to scream at her to move. Her skin seared with warning. She scrambled to stand and stumbled down the stairs, Bear leading the way. Her breaths came in short, rapid succession. She reached the barn door.

Outside, lightning lit up the sky, revealing a bone-chilling dark cloud swirling with madness, barreling down on the farm. Large. Ominous. Deadly.

Her chest tightened; her skin heated to boiling.

"Jolene!" She stumbled toward Hudson's muted voice.

A lawn chair slammed into her, sending her to the ground. Boards flew over her head. She clawed at the ground to regain her footing. Bear wouldn't leave her side.

"Go!" she yelled at him, but he wouldn't abandon her. Her hair lashed at her face. She couldn't find her breath, but she pushed up on her knees and shielded her eyes. Roots of a tree tore from the soil and it disappeared into the sky.

God. Help me, please, guide me through this storm.

Bear tugged the hem of her shirt.

Hudson yelled again, but she couldn't see anything; he sounded miles away.

Another flash of lightning revealed the ginormous tornado devouring the outer field and heading straight for the barn and house. A mass of lonely darkness barreled in on her—a living version of her greatest fear—and she'd be sucked into it if she didn't get to safety. But she couldn't even see the house or the barn.

Her gut churned and her legs trembled.

Bear kept pushing his nose hard against her side, so she followed him step by step by step, but the arms of the tornado pulled her back, hungry for whatever it could gobble up.

Her fingers found something hard, so she felt around and opened her eyes. Front porch steps. That gave her something to work with. At least she could get to an inner room. No way she'd make it to the storm shelter under the house. This was her best shot, and based on Bear's tugging and barking and nudging, he thought so, too. She climbed and climbed until she felt the door and ran her hand along the seam to the knob, shoved it open, crawled in and threw all her body weight into the door. She gasped and heaved.

Windows shattered.

She forced a breath into her lungs, but the dust and dirt filled her throat, making her cough.

Even with the windows blown out, she could

see a little better than when she was outside. Bear stood several feet away barking at her, so she kept her head low and raced for the hallway.

The roof ripped off with a roar. She hit the floor and looked up to a swirling madness of debris and wind.

She thought she heard Bear's muted bark but wasn't sure through the rumble. With all her strength, she crawled down the hall, but a chair blocked her path. Bear barked on the other side, guiding her in the darkness, so she scaled over and tumbled down next to Bear. Her hands shook, her body trembled.

Tub. It would be the safest place. But she never got the chance to move again.

The walls caved in around her.

And everything went dark.

Ace woke with his face pressed against the Bible to a loud, grinding sound in the distance. The hair on the back of his neck rose. That sound was one a person never forgot once they'd been near one.

Tornado.

He hobbled as fast as he could outside and waited for the flash of lightning to reveal the massive funnel of wind.

Headed straight for the Kenmore ranch.

His breath caught. Heart stopped. Blood drained, leaving a cold shiver deep inside him. The darkness pressed in from the edges of his vision.

"No, no, no."

In that moment, he envisioned his next night terror.

Not this time. This time he'd save them. He forced his breathing into submission, grabbed his cell phone and keys from the table and made it to his truck faster than he thought his leg could get him there.

Foot pressing the gas pedal to the floorboard, he raced down his drive chasing down the ashen swirl only a couple of miles away but yet so far. Too far to make it before the tornado reached Kenmore Ranch.

He fisted his hands and pounded the wheel. "Not this time. I won't let them die!" There was no way he'd fail Jolene, Bear and the Kenmores like he'd failed his men, like he'd failed Jimmy.

His heart hammered, pulse revved and an attack threatened. No. He wouldn't allow it. Not now. Fuzziness tried to choke his vision, but he remembered Jolene showing him how to breathe through it so he forced air into his lungs one breath at a time.

Gravel spit up from his tires; he jerked the

wheel and skidded onto the street. A barn door crashed into the road and broke apart, sending wood beams into the air. It smashed into the front of his truck, causing him to swerve, but he regained control. One of the headlights went out, his only means of seeing ahead, but he didn't care if something slammed into his truck. Life meant nothing without Jolene in this world. In his world.

Is that what You were trying to tell me, God? To love her the way she deserves, to accept her into my heart? "Save her, God, and I'll do whatever You want."

He turned down the road to their farm, fishtailing.

Lightning highlighted the thunderous threat barreling down on the farm. "No. No. No!" He gripped the steering wheel and hit the hill so fast it sent him airborne. When he came down on the other side, he saw the mass sucking up the last bits of the farm and carrying it away.

He skidded to a stop at the sight of the war zone that settled into heaping piles of wreckage. "Noooo!"

His hands shook so hard he struggled to open his door. When he did, he got out, only to crumple to the ground.

The side of the barn with the apartment had a

tree trunk sticking out of it, and the house was half-demolished, imploded in on itself.

"Move, soldier," he commanded himself. "Survivors." He clung to the hope that Jolene and Bear and the Kenmore family managed to ride out the storm and needed rescue, so he gripped the truck door, hauled himself up and headed to the barn first. A horse raced by him. The sound of a cow mooing gave him hope and energy to move forward, but his pulse in his ears remained as loud as that cloud that passed over them.

God, please. I'll do anything. I'll tell her how I feel, open my heart completely. Just let her live.

Inside the barn, the wooden stairs were broken in half. "Jolene! Bear!" he yelled, but there was no answer. A ladder on the wall remained along with a piece of paper still eerily sitting on the desk untouched.

He set the ladder up to reach the upper part of the stairs and, one rung at a time, managed to climb, rotating his hip to bring his prosthetic up each level until he was high enough to peer into the room.

A cat darted out, making him sway on the ladder. It nimbly maneuvered the stairs and hopped down to the ground. "Jolene? Bear?"

Nothing. He searched the small room, but the floor was crumbled, so he knew he couldn't climb up there. Through a hole in the wall, he could see the bathroom. No one was inside. Good.

No body meant hope.

He climbed down. His stomach churned, but he remembered the storm shelter under the house. Hopefully, they made it in time. Clinging to that kernel of hope, he maneuvered over a tractor on its side by straddling it and then yanking his prosthetic leg over. He made it to the shelter and realized why no one had come out. A wall had fallen in on it, leaving a heavy board over the opening.

"Anyone in there?" He pounded on the door.

Faint voices came through, followed by a return knock. "I'm going to get you out." He squatted, and while trying to maintain his balance, he used the leg strength he'd been working on to yank the board once. He fell on his backside but got back up and did it again and again and again until it finally tumbled off the door and he yanked it open.

Hudson crawled out. "Ace." Hudson swiped his hair out of his face and clapped him on the back. "Thank you."

"Everyone okay?" Ace asked, scanning the

small crawl space to find Juniper with Gracie in her arms.

No Jolene.

His body tensed. "Where's—"

Hudson helped Juniper and Gracie out. "I heard her yelling and Bear barking. Once I got Gracie and Juniper into the shelter, I was going to go back for them, but then the door slammed shut and I couldn't get out."

Gracie cried in her mother's arms; Juniper held the girl tightly to her chest, shielding her from the visible distraction.

Ace turned, eyeing the field, the barn, the house. He stumbled and fell, but Hudson offered him a hand. "We'll look for them together. They are both smart. I'm sure they found somewhere to ride out the storm."

Devastation appeared everywhere he turned. Where could they have ridden anything out? His heart cracked and shattered at the sight. The thought of losing Jolene stung all the way to his bones. No, to his soul.

"Woof. Woof."

Bear's bark drew him to the half-crumbled house. A hint of hope flittered into Ace's heart.

"Mommy, my room gone," Gracie cried.

"Don't worry, we can always rebuild," Juniper reassured the child.

"But my horse," Gracie whimpered.

Hudson eyed the house. "I'll find your stuffed horse, honey. Juniper, drive her to Mindi's. I'll call you when we have Jolene."

"No, go to my place. It's closer. It's unlocked and safe. Don't try to drive into town." Ace followed the bark until he found Bear on top of a pile of rubble. He rubbed the dog's ears. "Good to see you, boy. I missed you." He pressed a kiss to the dog's head. "Where's Jolene?"

Bear pawed at the wood beneath them. "Woof, Woof."

Ace collapsed and yanked a board and tossed it. Hudson joined him. Bear kept barking as if to tell Jolene to hold on.

Ace had seen this kind of destruction too much during the war and knew the chance of her survival was slim. If she lived, it would be a wonder that only God could provide.

He yanked a headboard and saw it. A hand. Dirty, bloodstained. But a hand. Jolene's hand.

His vision threatened to darken again but he forced it into submission.

Hudson dug in by his side and they carefully lifted wood and plaster and toys. "Jolene!" he yelled but no response.

An arm.

A hip.

Hair.

Piece by piece, they unveiled the most beautiful sight he'd ever seen. When they uncovered her chest, he took in a stuttered breath and pressed his ear to her heart.

Bu-bump. Bu-bump.

"She's alive," he yelled to Heaven, his throat tight with emotion.

The last bit of debris revealed her face and a gash on her forehead. "Jolene. I'm here. You're not alone. Wake up, honey. Wake up."

Nothing. Not even a flutter of an eyelid.

"We need to get her to the hospital," Ace said but looked at her mangled body and didn't know if they should move her. "Grab the door, there. We'll roll her onto it and I'll ride in the back of the truck with her. Emergency services might take too long to get here with the storm damage."

Hudson slid the door over on top of the mound. "One, two, three."

Supporting her head, they rolled her and slid the door under her, then lifted her. Ace fought for the strength and balance to maneuver over the debris, and he'd never wished so hard in his life that he would've done his therapy from day one because he needed it to save the woman he cared about most in this world.

They reached the truck and slid her into the back. "Keys are in the ignition. I'm staying back here with her. Drive fast but avoid any major jostling if you can help it."

Hudson nodded and hopped into the driver's seat. Ace collapsed into the truck, heaving for breath by her side. Bear hopped up next to him. "I'm here. You're not alone. I won't leave you no matter what. I'll never leave you again."

Bear placed a paw on his arm so Ace wrapped his arms around his furry friend. "You did good. I know you saved her when I wasn't here. You're the best friend a man could ever ask for. You have a forever home with me. I'm sorry I let you down."

The truck rumbled to life; he held her hand, willing her eyes to open. "You know, I've been reading your Bible. I think it made me feel closer to you since you've been gone, and I learned one thing. I'm a fool." He chuckled, thinking about how she'd agree with him on that.

He brushed her hair from her face and stroked her cheek. "You challenged me to be a better person, and I thought I'd tried, but I only pretended to be the person I thought you wanted for a time. But now, I promise if you open your eyes, I'll be the man you deserve." His voice broke. "Honey, please, the thought of you being in darkness shreds me. But I promise you one thing. I don't care if you're unconscious for a decade, I won't leave you. I'll get your Bible and I'll read to you all night, every night. You'll never be alone as long as I'm in your life. Because I realize something. The moment I thought you were gone…" His voice broke. His chest was so tight he thought it would squeeze his heart to goo. "I realized that I don't want to waste another moment away from you because whatever time God gives us, I will accept with grace and gratitude. Because, Jolene Pearl, you not only mended my heart, you *are* my heart. I love you."

"Love you, too." Her lips moved and he heard her whispered words despite the wind passing and the road noise.

"Woof."

"Jolene?" He collapsed onto his side and kissed her cheeks and nose and lips. "I'm here. You're not alone."

Her eyelids fluttered, but he could tell she fought for consciousness. "I know. And neither are you if you're truly willing to not run the next time life gets difficult."

"I promise." He grabbed her hand and held it to his lips. "If you'll have me, I'm all yours forever and always. I'll never leave you in the light or the darkness again."

Bear pawed them both as if to make his own vow.

They pulled into the hospital parking lot. "We're here. You're going to be fine."

"Promise me one thing," she said, holding tight to his hand. "If something happens and I don't—"

"You will." He couldn't even think of such a thing.

"If I don't, promise me you won't cut yourself off from the world again. Trust God that He has a plan."

He didn't want to consider that God's plan could include taking Jolene from him.

"Get her out and then onto the gurney," a man in scrubs hollered.

"Promise me." Jolene tried to lift her head but it thudded back against the door.

"I promise. For you, I'll never turn my back on the world again." And he meant it; if only in her name, he'd work hard to honor what she'd taught him. But more than anything, he wanted the chance to learn more in this life from Jolene. But he knew now that was up to God.

They ushered her away and Hudson looked at the sliding doors, then back at the truck.

Ace managed to stand, despite his trembling, weak legs. "Go be with your family, and if you would take Bear with you, please." He bent down and loved on Bear. "Sorry, buddy, no dogs allowed in the hospital, but I promise to take good care of our girl. You go home and get a steak. You've earned it." He stood and faced Hudson. "I promise to text you updates."

He nodded. "I'll be back after I check on them. Thanks for getting us out of there. Tell Jolene we're praying for her and we'll be back soon."

Ace went inside and filled out all the paperwork he could and waited and waited. Helpless, lost and broken. After pacing and asking and pacing some more, he went back to the desk. "Is there a chapel in the hospital?"

"Yes, third floor." The receptionist pointed to the elevators.

"If there's news?"

"We have your cell number, sir."

He went to the third floor; inside the chapel, he fell to his knees and prayed. Prayed for guidance, for hope, for Jolene. He prayed and prayed and prayed until his phone finally buzzed.

Chapter Twelve

Jolene woke to beeps and bleeps and the odor of antiseptic. She stiffened and wanted to scream, but then she heard Ace's voice.

Not just talking but reading the Bible to her the way he had that night while she slept. Everything ached from scalp to toes, but she managed to force her eyes open to a spinning room. She followed his voice and turned her head to find a scruffy, bearded Ace hunched, talking with a hoarse voice. How long had he been there?

She reached for him, but the wire attached to her finger and the IV in her arm restricted her movement. "Hey," she said, but her dry throat didn't allow any volume. She tried to sit up but only managed to rise onto one elbow before she collapsed.

Ace shut the Bible and stood, taking her hand. "You're awake."

She looked up at his dirt-stained red eyes. "How long have I been out?"

"Two excruciatingly long days," he choked out, tears filling his eyes.

"You've been here all that time reading to me, haven't you?"

He only nodded. "I'll never leave you again." He kissed her knuckles and rested his forehead gently against hers. "I'm so sorry, Jolene."

"It wasn't your fault. It was a tornado."

He sat back and ran his thumb over her cheek. "No, that I couldn't help. I'm sorry for abandoning you when we got so close it scared me. But I learned one important lesson when I thought you were gone."

"What's that?" she asked, her own emotions bubbling to the surface, tightening her throat.

"That every second God allows me to be with you is a gift and I'd be a fool not to embrace such a glorious chance in this life." He studied her face, her arms, and then looked back at her. "Are you in a lot of pain?"

"Just achy and thirsty."

He grabbed a cup with a straw, then slid his hand behind her head to help her lift enough to take a few swallows. The cold soothed her throat.

"Nurse said you could have water when you woke up and to call her if you need something. I'll get her." He set the cup on a tray, but she didn't release him; she never wanted to let him go again.

"No, I don't like the medications. Not since I recovered from Guillain-Barré. And the pain's not so bad." Memories filtered in, causing her pulse to bleep the machine faster. "Hudson, Juniper, Gracie?"

"Relax. All fine."

"Bear?"

Ace kissed her hand and held it to his chest. "He's resting at my place with Hudson and Jolene and Gracie."

She allowed the tension to leave her neck and lay back against the pillow. "The house. That beautiful old farmhouse." She sucked in a stuttered breath at the thought.

"They're just thankful you all made it through alright. Apparently, there was a problem with the early warning system. The town council is reaching out to the county."

"Bear saved my life. Led me through the darkness to the house."

"He's special, but he misses you. They said he sits in the corner whining most of the time."

"Where is everybody going to stay during the rebuild? Will we be able to continue the hippotherapy program? What about Bear's paperwork and the fall festival?"

"Slow down," Ace chuckled. "The rebuild will take a while, and you need to heal before you go back to work. You have some fractured ribs, broken toes and a head injury. The festival was postponed by two weeks, so if you're good and rest up, maybe we'll be able to take Bear for the final test."

She took in a deep breath. "It's really all gone, isn't it?"

"Nothing that can't be fixed. In the meantime, Hudson's already clearing out my office to put in a bed for Logan, who's also going to be arriving soon. We'll have a full house."

"We?" She yawned, sleep claiming her once more.

"Shh, rest. We'll talk later. The quicker you get better, the quicker we get out of here. Don't worry, I'll keep reading to you while you sleep."

"No." She squeezed his hand.

He blinked at her, but he faded in and out with each blink. "No, you need sleep."

"I told you I'm never going to leave you again."

"I know." She swallowed and tried to smile. "But I'm not scared anymore because I know I'm not alone."

Hudson showed up for long enough to discuss logistics and brought Ace a change of clothes, but after a quick shower, Ace climbed onto the reclining chair and took a nap by Jolene. For the next two days, he didn't leave Jolene's side. He only left when they started talking about her release; he had to finish getting the downstairs living room ready for Logan and the office-turned-guest-room on the main floor for Jolene so she didn't have to climb the stairs either.

He didn't like leaving her there, but Mindi wanted to visit and Hudson took up a shift, too.

Juniper helped him choose some bedding and new clothes for Jolene since most of her stuff had been destroyed by the tornado and rain, and the apartment wasn't safe to get up into until the floor could be reinforced.

He checked on Bear, but he remained in his spot, unmoving, eyeing the front door as if he would wilt away if Jolene didn't come home soon. Ace could relate to that.

A car pulled up out front, so he headed outside to discover Benjamin walking up the front steps. "I came by to let you know that I'm selling my land in between you and the Kenmore property. There isn't much left of my house, and I've decided to move into town. The place doesn't have any meaning to me since my wife passed."

Ace saw Benjamin in a different light and felt convicted for judging him all this time. "Listen,

I have a huge house here. If you need a place to stay, I have one extra room left, but I warn you it'll be busy around here."

He tilted his head and narrowed his gaze, then shook his head. "Why would you offer me that? I tried to have that dog put down, cut your fence and hunted on your land."

"Why did you do that?"

The man shrugged. "Honestly, I think I wanted to make everyone else as miserable as I am, or maybe I wanted to find some reason to interact with people. Gets lonely on the farm alone. Stupid, I know." He took a tentative step closer and offered his hand. "I am sorry."

"So am I," Ace said, then shook Benjamin's hand. "You're welcome here anytime you want. Come for dinner, coffee or just to chat. And the offer stands. It'll be crowded here, so you won't be able to find a way to be lonely."

"Thanks for the offer, but I'm going to try to open a shop in town once I figure a few things out. My son's always telling me I need to do what I enjoy and maybe I'd find some way to move on."

"What kind of shop?" Ace asked, wanting the man to feel like he was interested in having him as a friend.

Benjamin eyed the front porch, the windows on the second floor, the bush at the railing. "Yarn store."

Ace fought his smile because he could tell the man was serious.

"I know it sounds crazy. A forty-year-old man who can't carry on a civil conversation wanting to teach people how to knit and crochet. But I learned in order to help Natalie with her knitting when she started having issues with her hands. And when she passed away, I missed her so much, and I couldn't bear to see her half-finished projects left behind, so I spent weeks finishing everything she had in the house. Then I heard there was a need for newborn caps, so I knitted those and sent them to the hospital. And the women's shelter in Atlanta. I made some kids' sweaters. I thought I'd name the shop Natalie Knits."

"That sounds like an excellent idea." Ace offered an encouraging smile.

Hudson's truck turned down the long drive and Ace spotted Jolene in the passenger seat. He couldn't help himself but to rush past Benjamin to take Jolene into his arms. "What are you doing here? You weren't supposed to be released until tomorrow. I would've been there."

Bear flew out of the house and danced around them barking.

"They mentioned I could leave, and no offense, but I wasn't waiting for you to come get me. Hudson gave me a ride here to see you. Mindi says I can stay with her for some time."

"Woof. Woof."

"I missed you, too, buddy." She leaned far enough to scratch his ears, her ribs obviously still bothering her.

Ace opened his mouth, but Benjamin waved a goodbye, drawing him to one more task. "Hey, wait up. I still have your shotgun. The police officer left it here that day and you'd gone before I could return it to you." He took Jolene by the elbow. "Let me get her settled and I'll get it for you."

Jolene waved him away from her once she made it to the top front porch step. "Go, I'll wait here. I'd like some fresh air for a minute after being cooped up in the hospital for so long."

Ace hurried to the cabinet, snagged the gun and met Benjamin back outside.

"Not sure I have a use for this anymore, but I know my son would like me to send it to him." Benjamin took the gun, slung it over his shoulder and headed down the stairs as Jolene shuffled toward the house.

Bear erupted and vaulted off the steps, tumbling, but recovered and leaped onto Benjamin.

Jolene gasped from the top step.

"No!" Ace yelled.

Benjamin stayed on the ground, eyes closed, hands up by his ears.

Bear snarled and snapped, and then Ace had an idea. "Stay still."

"Not moving," Benjamin whispered out the side of his mouth.

Ace bent over and slid the gun away from him. "Down, boy."

Bear jumped off and settled next to Ace's side.

"It's the gun. That's his trigger," Ace announced. "I can't believe I didn't think about that before."

"I had my suspicion, but this proves it. But I don't think it's just the gun, it's anything that reminds him of the night his handler was killed." Jolene lit up. "You're not trying to attack anyone. You're trying to save people like you were trained to do. He isn't dangerous, he just needs to be retrained."

She took Ace's hand, lowered by Bear's side and petted him. "You're a good boy. You're a rescue dog."

He popped up, his ears straighter than Ace had ever seen them. "I think you found your new career there, little man."

Bear stood up on all three legs, wagging his tail, and ran over to Benjamin, licking his face.

He laughed and sat up, shooing Bear away. "I'm not sure anymore if he wants to lick me or bite me."

"No gun, he's gonna love you. He's a lover," Jolene said. "I think we're ready for our final test, and I can turn in the paperwork. I hear the fall festival's in two days."

Ace shook his head. "You can't—"

"Oh, no you don't. I'm going to that festival because I need to help out with the money collection for the food pantry donations."

"You're not going to run yourself into the ground helping other people until you're better," Ace demanded, but at the sideways glance, he already knew he'd have a big battle on his hands.

She gave him that I'm-gonna-win look. "I can go back to helping out at the kids' table if you prefer."

"No, you sitting, helping by collecting money with me, is the only way you're going."

Jolene nodded. "Agreed. You know I'll never stop volunteering, but I can promise you one thing. I won't put it before you."

Ace took her into his arms. "That's good to know, but I think I'll just have to be your assistant."

"I can live with that." Jolene bit her bottom lip. "Maybe the fall festival can be our official first date."

"Why wait until tomorrow?"

She shrugged. "I need to go get some clothes and get settled at Mindi's. I just came by to say hi."

Hudson shrugged as if he wasn't going to get into the conversation of where Jolene would be staying. "I'm going to go pick up Juniper—she's been going through some things at the ranch—and then we're headed to town to get Gracie from Mindi's. We'll grab some ice cream before we return."

Benjamin cleared his throat. "I need to go, too. Got to start clearing out my own wreckage."

Ace nodded. "Listen, I'll come by once Jolene's settled to help you, and Hudson and I can discuss the purchase of your property. Figure out what your number is, and we'll talk about it."

Hudson lifted his brows. "Property's for sale?"

"Yeah, I'll catch you up on that at dinner tonight," Ace said, but shifted his attention, took Jolene by the hand and headed for the house, excited to show her the room he'd set up for her downstairs.

Bear trotted inside in front of them with tail high and prancing about like a show dog. "You don't need to go shopping right away. Juniper helped me, and we set this up." He opened the guest room door to show her the room he'd arranged for her.

She smiled up at him but he saw in her eyes there was a problem.

"If you don't like it, I can change anything." He helped her to the bed and sat her down, opening drawers. "Juniper picked out the clothes and stuff. I just set everything up."

"It's perfect, thank you. But—"

"But what?"

"I can't stay here."

"Why not?"

She toed the powder blue rug at her feet. "It's not appropriate, Ace. Not if we want to date."

He let out a laugh, but she looked up at him with a quizzical gaze. "What's funny?"

"I'm not planning on dating you, hon."

She opened her mouth but shut it.

"Come with me." He went to the living room and pointed out the window at the barn. "I'll be staying there so you don't have to worry about being appropriate."

"Mindi—"

"No way. You're staying here with all of us.

You'll need to work hard to get the hippotherapy program back up and running, and staying here makes that easier due to the close proximity of the Kenmore ranch. Not to mention Hudson, Juniper and Gracie living here will make it convenient for you guys to work."

"I can't let you live out there while we take over your house."

"I'm not planning on living there long."

She blinked up at him. She still didn't get it, so he took her in his arms and cupped her cheeks, nudging her to look up to him. His pulse hammered with the thought of her rejection, but he wouldn't let that stop him. "Let me be clear. I don't want to date you because dating's to figure out how you feel about someone, and I already know how I feel. I love you. And I want to spend the rest of my life with you."

He kissed her. Not a peck on the lips, but the kind of kiss that would tell her he wanted her forever and always, as long as God blessed them with time together.

Chapter Thirteen

The farm spun around Jolene. Ace was kissing her.

His strong lips claimed hers with intent, sending her pulse revving to two hundred horsepower.

It was a kiss she'd been waiting for her entire life. The kind movies were made about, and books were written to try to capture that toe-curling, happily-ever-after feeling. But in that moment, she realized all those fictional tales fell short because kissing Ace shattered every thought she ever had of what a kiss could be.

She wrapped her arms around his neck and held on so she wouldn't collapse from the intense emotions surging through her. Not even the pain in her ribs made her pull away.

When they parted, they were both breathless. She slid down to her toes before she realized he'd even lifted her. The cracked ribs screamed at her, but she didn't care because kissing Ace healed her deepest wounds.

"Wow," he whispered, leaning down and resting his head and nose to hers.

"Yeah, wow." His heart pounded so hard she could feel it beating against her chest. "I love you, too."

"That's good because I have a question to ask you." He stood straight and looked down at her.

"Yes?"

"Not now. Fall's your favorite, so I have a plan."

She wanted to tell him she didn't care about any plan, she'd say yes, but at his silly grin, she wanted to give this to him. When Ace made a plan, she knew he was serious.

"Besides, we probably need to officially go on that first real date. If you'll still go with me to the fall festival, I think I might find the right time to ask you my question."

She shivered at the idea. Could he really mean to ask her to marry him? That would be insane. Sure, they'd known each other for several months, but only really got to know each other in the last month or so.

But those weeks turned into months when the fall festival was postponed until almost Thanksgiving.

The town was understandably still sensitive to the weather, and the slightest breeze caused the council to reschedule. Not to mention the people rebuilding made finding volunteers with free time difficult. But the day finally came. And she'd made a full recovery, swapping back to a volunteer position at the children's table at the festival.

True to his word, Ace remained out in the barn, where he'd go every night after a goodnight kiss on the front porch.

Logan was due to arrive in a few days, his plans delayed by red tape at the VA and transferring his benefits to see someone in Georgia. But she'd hoped to help with his rehabilitation while waiting on the last of the barn construction to be finished at the Kenmore ranch. Hudson had spent day in and day out at their place working to rebuild while Juniper worked tending animals, and what crops had survived the storm they harvested and drove to Atlanta.

They were blessed not to be strapped for money, but they all were ready to return to some sort of normalcy.

Ace pulled into a parking space in town and stole another kiss before walking around the truck to let her and Bear out. "You ready, boy? Final test."

"Good. I'm ready to not have to worry about animal control appearing to take him away."

Ace took her hand, sending a tingle up her arm. Would he really propose today or had she invented this in her head? A family, one that didn't run off, would be amazing, but she would wait however long it took. Because it would happen in God's time.

"And he's perked up since you've moved back." Ace scanned the parking lot, then gave her a peck on the cheek. "His certification came in this morning. Bear is on his way to becoming a certified rescue animal. Thanks to his K-9 status, Sheriff Monroe has fast-tracked him. I've passed my written exams and Bear even passed two of his SARTECH evaluations and temperament tests."

"Did you hear that, Bear? You have a new career."

"Woof!"

"Let's go. Got some volunteering to do." He walked with her up the sidewalk wearing his blue shirt she loved so much, holding Bear's leash.

They weaved through the crowd of Willow Oaks residents. Little Jimmy charged for them with his parents by his side. "Giant!"

Ace lowered to a squat and opened his arms to Jimmy, who hobbled over with his canes.

Jolene stood to the side to let Ace swoop him up in the air and then set him down. The two of them had gotten close doing therapy together.

"How's the bravest boy I know doing? I hear you're going to be one of my first riding clients once Ms. Jolene releases you from therapy."

"Yes, and I promise to follow all the directions." Jimmy hugged him tight around his neck.

"And I promise not to run off if you get hurt." Ace set him down. "Deal?" He offered his hand and Jimmy shook it.

"Deal." They fist-bumped and Dad shook Ace's hand.

"I'll be helping Ms. Jolene at the painting table, so make sure to stop by to see us later."

Jimmy nodded but didn't hang long before he shot off with a bright smile toward the ball toss booth.

"He's come a long way," Jolene said to his mother.

"Thanks to the two of you." She offered the sweetest smile, then trotted after her son, who moved faster than the kids without canes. Soon he'd be out of the braces and off on two legs.

Ace took her hand once more and they walked through the main row of games. Benjamin Snyder waved from the dunking booth seat. "Did I mention I'm going to be at a knitting class this weekend?" Jolene asked, hoping he'd want to join her like he had for the assistive pet trainer classes, the sailing class on the lake and the painting class.

"You know, when I encouraged you to find a hobby, I didn't mean you had to try all of them."

She hip-bumped him. "I haven't tried all of them. Oh, but there's a pickleball—"

He pulled her in for a kiss. Not the knee-weakening kind but it felt like the sun cast a shine over her. "Stop. No more. You have enough hobbies now."

She shrugged, but they both laughed and went to work helping anyone and everyone who needed it. The weather had turned chillier than anticipated but thankfully they didn't cancel the festival again because in a few days, they'd be putting up the Christmas tree in the square and planning their Christmas fair.

The leaves were blown down, providing the kids with a natural game to play, jumping in and kicking them around under the large oak tree in the center of town.

Children. She'd never imagined having any of her own, but if she did, she'd want to raise them without nannies. It would be a balance to figure out how to continue working and being a mother, but Juniper did it and Gracie got all the love and attention she needed.

Seated at the kids' craft table, she opened up the paints and set them out for those kids who wanted to paint and arranged hers on the small table at her side for face painting. She waited for her first participant when she spotted Hudson and Ace over by the jumpy house.

Juniper joined Jolene with Gracie, who picked up a paintbrush. "I paint?"

"Sure." Juniper smiled brightly at the big milestone. Gracie never wanted to hold anything but the reins of a pony.

Gracie stuck her tongue out the side of her mouth and picked up the paintbrush in a fisted hand. Juniper looked at Jolene, who shook her head and whispered, "Let this be fun, correction later."

She nodded and the first kiddo stepped up. "Butterfly?" The little girl pointed at her cheek.

"Sure, honey." Jolene painted her best version, and to her surprise, it looked pretty good.

"You nervous?" Juniper asked.

"Petrified, if I'm being honest." She chuckled.

Juniper patted her arm. "You could say no. It hasn't been that long. Tell him you need time."

"No, not because of that. Because I want to

marry him. But he might not ask. As you said, it hasn't been that long."

Juniper leaned in close. "I saw him showing Hudson something in a small box."

Fizzles of energy bubbled under her skin. "Really?"

"Yeah, I didn't see what was inside, but I'm pretty sure it was a ring."

Bear trotted over along with the animal control administrator. "Why is this dog not on a leash?"

Jolene's world shattered. "I, um...sorry." She looked where Ace stood moments ago but didn't spot him. *How had Bear ended up off-leash?* "I'll make sure to get him on a leash immediately. Listen, I'm glad you're here. I have all the documentation."

She took the folder out of her purse and handed it to the man. "As you can see, we've determined that he doesn't actually have a trigger, but that he uses his police training when he hears a loud sound that indicates danger or when he sees a gun. We are retraining him and he's doing well. Mr. Snyder wrote a letter attesting to how well Bear is doing and withdrew his complaint. Also, there is documentation that he not only rescued me but assisted in locating several other people after the tornado.

He's even completed his temperament test and passed several evaluations so he's on his way to becoming a search and rescue animal."

"Ms. Pearl, I'll review the paperwork, but where is his tag? I'm going to have to take him in and you'll need to come to the pound with his tags to retrieve him."

"No, he has tags. Look." Jolene bent down and spotted a shiny ring tied to his collar.

"Woof. Woof."

Jolene's hands trembled, but she managed to untie the string and sit up to find Ace down on one knee next to Bear. He took the ring from her. "Jolene Pearl, I did try to reach your father but he didn't return my calls, so I asked the next best thing, Hudson, who considers himself your brother. He granted me the honor, and so I kneel before you a broken man who you've put back together with the help of God."

His voice trembled, and she wanted to tell him yes to save him from any more emotional strain, but he took her hand. "We might not have been dating long, like an hour," he chuckled.

She tried to stop her fingers from shaking but she couldn't because her entire body was about ready to jump out of the chair.

"But in the short time we've been together, I know with certainty that I have never loved a woman the way I love you. You make the world brighter, troubles easier, and you brought joy into my heart like I've never known. What I'm trying to ask is, will you be my wife?"

Tears slid down her face; she let out a choked, "Yes."

He slid the ring on and she flung herself into his arms, but he didn't fall; he stood and held her the way she knew he would the rest of their days.

Cheers sounded. Gracie threw herself into their sides and hugged them tight. "I be flower girl."

Bear barked.

"Yes, you can be ring bearer. You did well," Ace said.

The animal control guy cleared his throat. "Here's the signed paperwork. And I wish you all the best."

"Woof."

"Even you, Bear." The man rubbed the sweet dog's head.

The crowd dispersed. But Ace didn't leave her side. He even helped paint kids' faces.

"What do you think about a Christmas wedding?" Ace asked while dotting Dalmatian spots onto a little boy's face.

"Why so quick?" Jolene asked, but was eager to agree.

"It's going to get cold in that barn," he teased.

She dipped her paintbrush in water. "I see how important our marriage is to you."

The kiddos heard the call for cake and took off, so he turned her to face him. "I want to get married because every precious moment I can have with you, I don't want to waste. Because I promised God that I would never leave you, and I intend to keep that promise."

Jolene nodded. "I don't want anything fancy." And in that moment, she saw how God had worked wonders in Ace Gatlin, teaching him how to open his heart wide enough to love not only her but so many around him. "But I think a Christmas wedding is perfect."

* * * * *

If you enjoyed this K9 Companions book, don't miss An Unexpected Christmas Helper *by* New York Times *bestselling author Lee Tobin McClain, coming next month from Love Inspired!*

Dear Readers,

Working with veterans during my time at the Veterans Admiration Hospital was one of the most eye-opening and humbling experiences of my life. It gave me the privilege of seeing not only their courage and resilience but also the struggles they face daily—struggles that many of us may never fully understand. I've always carried the hope of one day sharing their stories, giving readers a glimpse into their world and the challenges they navigate after serving our country.

That hope grew even stronger when, at a book signing, I met a remarkable police K-9 missing a leg after being shot in the line of duty. This incredible dog was calm and determined, embodying the same quiet heroism I'd seen in so many veterans. But what struck me even more was learning about the difficult reality some service and K-9 dogs face when they lose their handlers or are injured. Due to limited resources and funding, many of these dogs are left without homes or even euthanized because they no longer "fit" into the systems they once served so loyally.

That moment stayed with me, blending two worlds close to my heart: the veterans I worked with and the service animals who serve alongside them. It inspired me to write this story—a tale that gives a voice to these heroes, both human and canine.

Sincerely,
Ciara

Get up to 4 Free Books!

We'll send you 2 free books from each series you try PLUS a free Mystery Gift.

FREE Value Over $25

Both the **Love Inspired®** and **Love Inspired® Suspense** series feature compelling novels filled with inspirational romance, faith, forgiveness and hope.

YES! Please send me 2 FREE novels from the Love Inspired or Love Inspired Suspense series and my FREE gift (gift is worth about $10 retail). After receiving them, if I don't wish to receive any more books, I can return the shipping statement marked "cancel." If I don't cancel, I will receive 6 brand-new Love Inspired Larger-Print books or Love Inspired Suspense Larger-Print books every month and be billed just $7.19 each in the U.S. or $7.99 each in Canada. That is a savings of 20% off the cover price. It's quite a bargain! Shipping and handling is just 50¢ per book in the U.S. and $1.25 per book in Canada.* I understand that accepting the 2 free books and gift places me under no obligation to buy anything. I can always return a shipment and cancel at any time by calling the number below. The free books and gift are mine to keep no matter what I decide.

Choose one:
☐ **Love Inspired Larger-Print** (122/322 BPA G36Y)
☐ **Love Inspired Suspense Larger-Print** (107/307 BPA G36Y)
☐ **Or Try Both!** (122/322 & 107/307 BPA G36Z)

Name (please print)

Address   Apt. #

City   State/Province   Zip/Postal Code

Email: Please check this box ☐ if you would like to receive newsletters and promotional emails from Harlequin Enterprises ULC and its affiliates. You can unsubscribe anytime.

Mail to the Harlequin Reader Service:
IN U.S.A.: P.O. Box 1341, Buffalo, NY 14240-8531
IN CANADA: P.O. Box 603, Fort Erie, Ontario L2A 5X3

Want to explore our other series or interested in ebooks? Visit www.ReaderService.com or call 1-800-873-8635.

---

*Terms and prices subject to change without notice. Prices do not include sales taxes, which will be charged (if applicable) based on your state or country of residence. Canadian residents will be charged applicable taxes. Offer not valid in Quebec. This offer is limited to one order per household. Books received may not be as shown. Not valid for current subscribers to the Love Inspired or Love Inspired Suspense series. All orders subject to approval. Credit or debit balances in a customer's account(s) may be offset by any other outstanding balance owed by or to the customer. Please allow 4 to 6 weeks for delivery. Offer available while quantities last.

Your Privacy—Your information is being collected by Harlequin Enterprises ULC, operating as Harlequin Reader Service. For a complete summary of the information we collect, how we use this information and to whom it is disclosed, please visit our privacy notice located at https://corporate.harlequin.com/privacy-notice. Notice to California Residents – Under California law, you have specific rights to control and access your data. For more information on these rights and how to exercise them, visit https://corporate.harlequin.com/california-privacy. For additional information for residents of other U.S. states that provide their residents with certain rights with respect to personal data, visit https://corporate.harlequin.com/other-state-residents-privacy-rights/.

LIRLIS25